Archer's Sin

A Hearts and Thrones Novella

Amy Raby

Publisher's Note: This is a work of fiction. Names, characters, places, and incidents are a product of the author's imagination. Locales and public names are sometimes used for atmospheric purposes. Any resemblance to actual people, living or dead, or to businesses, companies, events, institutions, or locales is completely coincidental.

Book Layout ©2013 BookDesignTemplates.com

Archer's Sin/ Amy Raby. -- 1st ed.
ISBN 978-1-940987-01-9

ALSO BY AMY RABY

The Hearts and Thrones series

Assassin's Gambit
Spy's Honor
Prince's Fire

Triferian

Nalica wasn't used to crowds.

In the eastern mountains where she'd grown up, the air was thin and the trees were sparse, and one could walk all day without seeing another soul. Here at the festival grounds in Riat, the air tasted as thick as porridge, and she'd seen more people in an hour than she normally saw all year.

More than one pair of eyes lit on her as she walked. Her height made her stand out; she towered above most southern Kjallans. But they also looked askance at her unpowdered face and at the leathers she wore in lieu of a syrtos. And at the longbow she carried on her back.

Somewhere on the grounds was the registration for the Triferian archery tournament. She'd come a long way to enter because this tournament offered an unusual prize: after three days of competition, the winner would be granted a position as a prefect in the Riat City Guard. Nalica would give anything for a steady job and an opportunity to use her skills. She wanted that job. She would enter the tournament, and she would win it.

She squinted at a sign with a bow and arrow on it. Unlike many eastern Kjallans, she did know her letters, but she'd learned them late, and only just enough to get through her education in magic. Painstakingly, she worked out the words. The sign said when and where the three rounds of competition would take place, but it didn't say where to sign up. The only other sign in the area was one announcing a horse race.

The festival didn't officially start until tomorrow, which meant the crowds would get worse between now and then. On her left, merchant families raised tents. On her right, a group of men measured out an open field, planting flags in the ground as markers.

There, just ahead—a longbow bounced through the crowd on the back of a tall, burly man. Surely that man was here for the tournament. She hurried after him in case he knew where he was going. If he didn't, at least they'd be lost together.

She realized as she pushed her way toward him that he was *very* tall. It made him easy to follow, and she felt a certain kinship with him based solely on height.

The crowd thinned. She dodged around a few slow-moving people and was about to call out to him when he joined a group of men, all of them with longbows on their backs.

Well, this was fortunate. Someone here would know where to register for the tournament.

A black-haired archer with a sharp nose turned to greet the giant. The two clasped wrists and began to talk.

Nalica approached the group. "Sorry to jig in, but—"

"*Jig in*?" repeated the black-haired man.

Oops, that was an eastern phrase. What did southerners say? "Sorry to speak out of turn—"

"Is she speaking Kjallan, or is that some other language?" asked a man in a leather cap.

Nalica sighed inwardly. She had an accent, but it wasn't strong—at least she didn't think it was. She did tend to forget about those eastern phrases that weren't used in the south.

"Pay him no mind," the giant said to her. "He understands you perfectly well."

She looked up at him—in itself a novel act; so rarely did she look *up* to anybody—and nearly gasped. He was eastern Kjallan, and she'd bet her last quintetral he was from the mountains of the province of Vereth, same as she. His height and size ought to have tipped her off, but now that she saw him up close, his beard clinched it. Southern Kjallans shaved; her people did not. The giant's broad nose and features looked vaguely familiar. She might have seen him before, or more likely she'd met one of his family members. Clan identity was important in Vereth.

Southern Kjallans looked refined and fancy to her eyes, like toys rather than men. But this fellow was genuine, of true mountain stock. Her eyes traveled eagerly over his form. He wasn't just tall, but broad. Some might call him fat, but they'd be mistaken. The weight he carried was all muscle.

"That your daddy's bow?" asked the black-haired archer.

"No," said Nalica, drawing herself to her full height.

Black Hair snorted. "That's a six-foot longbow. You can't even string it."

"Do you think I'd carry a bow I couldn't string?" In fact, she could string it with or without her war magic. Many war mage archers couldn't handle their bows without calling upon their magically enhanced strength, but she could.

"Show me," he said.

Her shoulder twitched, and she almost reached for the bow. But she resisted the temptation. If she strung her bow as an exhibition for this sneering twit, she would only worsen her standing among the group. Even if she succeeded in stringing it, which of course she would, she would have allowed him to order her around. He would have made her perform like a trained dog while appointing himself arbiter of her performance. "If you want to see me string this bow, you can wait for the tournament like everyone else."

The other men chuckled—all but the giant, who regarded her gravely.

"I'll bet she can string it," said Leather Cap. "Look at those shoulders—you don't get muscles like that scrubbing pots in a scullery."

"I shouldn't be surprised she wants to enter the tournament," said Black Hair. "Justien, do all your eastern Kjallan females look like she-bears?"

Justien—that was the giant's name. She ignored the insult from the black-haired man. She'd heard worse.

"Strong women bear strong sons," said Justien. "It's a lesson you should learn, Caellus. It's not like you have much of value to pass on yourself."

The giant had only the slightest hint of an accent. Probably he'd left the east a long time ago.

Caellus snorted. "I'll stick to women who look like women. But Justien, you should propose marriage straight away. Who else but a walking she-bear could carry your child?"

Justien frowned.

Nalica had borne enough of this. Trading insults was not a skill she enjoyed or excelled at; she'd rather show these men up at the tournament. "Where's the registration?"

"You're wasting your time," said Caellus. "The tournament is special this year. War mages only."

"I savvy it," said Nalica.

"You what?" said Caellus.

"Three gods, we don't speak *savage*," said Leather Cap.

"I mean, I *know* it," said Nalica.

"So you're not entering?" said Caellus.

His question suggested he couldn't process the obvious conclusion that she was a war mage. She waited in silence to see if the others would figure it out. She knew they'd begun to entertain the possibility when some of them glanced at her neck, looking for her riftstone. They wouldn't be able to see it; the stone hung on a steel chain and was hidden beneath her shirt.

Caellus, apparently putting two and two together at last, turned to his fellows. "I hate it when people give top-tier riftstones to women. What a waste."

Leather Cap nodded. "I've a friend whose parents couldn't afford a stone."

"What's the real waste," put in Justien, "is when they give them to talentless hacks. Right, Caellus?"

A few chuckles broke the tension.

"It's not funny," said Caellus. "We shoot the first day without magic. Do you think she can get even one arrow on the butts without the magic doing the work for her?"

Justien grinned. "If she gets anything on the butts, she'll be shooting better than you."

More laughter from the group. Caellus glowered.

Nalica addressed Justien directly, figuring he was the only one who might give her a straight answer. "Sir, do you know where the registration is?"

"Of course. I'll show you the tent." He took her arm and led her away from the group.

As they walked in silence across the outskirts of the fairgrounds, Nalica felt hotly aware of his hand on her arm, a sensation that drove out all others. If there was a crowd around them, she was oblivious. If her feet were sore from walking all day, she felt no pain. Her entire awareness had narrowed to Justien's hand where it rested lightly on her flesh.

She was burning with questions she wanted to ask. What clan was he from? How long had he been away from eastern Kjall? Did he have family here? A wife? Probably no wife, given what Caellus had said. Never mind; she couldn't ask Justien any of this. Curious as she was, those questions were too personal. She'd only just met the man.

"What's your name?" asked Justien.

"Nalica," she said. "Are you in the tournament yourself?"

"Yes," said Justien. "Already registered. Allow me to warn you, Nalica, before you give the tournament director your money: I intend to win."

She smiled at him thinly. "Intentions are not reality."

"In this case, I think they will be." There was not a trace of humor or smugness in his voice. He acted as if he were simply sharing information. "I can outshoot anyone here, including you. I need that job in the city guard, and I intend to have it."

Nalica kept walking and said nothing. Justien had no idea how well she could shoot; he might well believe his claim that he was certain to win, but she knew it was an idle boast. She needed the city guard job too, probably more than he did. And she'd come to Riat for the sole purpose of winning it.

Justien took a somewhat roundabout route to the registration tent, knowing that when they reached it, he and this intriguing woman would have to part ways. He knew so little about her, but he was intensely curious. How rare it was to run into someone from his homeland! And a woman besides. He had to talk to her at least a little before he let her go.

"Is this your first Triferian?" he asked.

"My first in Riat."

Of course; he should have known better than to ask such a silly question. It was celebrated everywhere, just not in so grandiose a fashion as it was here at the imperial seat. He was flustered and showing it. How personal a question could he ask? He was dying to know what clan she was from. She could only be the daughter of a lord. There was no other explanation for her bearing a topaz, the rare and valuable riftstone of a war mage.

He forced himself to be patient. They'd be in the tournament for three days together; he'd have plenty of opportunity to get to know her. "How do you like the city so far?"

She paused before replying, and he could tell she was thinking about her answer before she spoke.

"It's different," she said. "I'm not used to all the people and noise."

"Riat's not normally this crowded," he said.

She smiled. "I suppose I threw myself into this head first, coming during the Triferian. Riat is a lot to take in, but it's a beautiful city—a prosperous city. I feel a sense of optimism here that I haven't felt in a decade."

"I know exactly what you mean." He'd left home long ago because there simply wasn't anything left for him in the east. No jobs, no money. Only the remnants of his family.

Gods, that smile of hers. He couldn't believe the other archers had jeered at her. Yes, she was a big woman, tall and strong. Yes, she looked out of place in southern Kjall. But a big, strong woman was no curiosity to him. He'd grown up around women just like her. Nalica was the first real woman he'd seen in a long time. And she was beautiful.

"You seem to have adapted well," she said.

"I've been here ten years now—not just Riat, but all around the south and up as far as Riorca. Mostly lost my accent, but I kept this." He touched his beard.

She rewarded him with that smile again.

"Nice bow you've got there," he said. "It's yew, isn't it? Did you make it yourself?"

"Of course. What proper archer doesn't make her own bow?"

"You'd be surprised. Lots of southern Kjallans think you're better off finding a good bowyer."

She shook her head. "The bow's got to fit the archer, and only the archer herself knows exactly how she wants it. You made yours, didn't you?"

"Certainly." He was of the same mind. Bowyers were capable of fine work, but an expert archer needed a custom weapon with just the right width and draw strength and flexibility. For that, the archer had to make his own.

They'd arrived at the registration tent; he couldn't delay her any longer. "The clerk's in there." He pointed. "See the guard insignia?"

"I savvy it. Thanks for your help." She headed into the tent.

He wanted to follow her but forced himself to turn around and walk away. Much as he wanted to get to know her, she was competition. Probably not strong competition, but who knew? She hadn't seemed intimidated by his claim that he was certain to win. Perhaps she was a better shot than he assumed. If so, all the more reason he should keep his distance. He needed that job in the city guard, and they could not both win. One of them or the other was going to be disappointed three days from now.

Inside the tent, Nalica found a thin-faced clerk sitting at a desk. He glanced at her and then returned to his paperwork.

She approached the desk. "I'm here to enter the archery tournament."

He looked up again, brows raised, and gave a deprecating laugh. "Actually, there's no need to register. The archery event is on Soldier's Day, and all you have to do is show up. We provide the bows, the arrows, and the targets." His eyes went to the bow that hung over her shoulder. "Or you can bring your own, I suppose."

"That's not the event I'm talking about," she said. "I'm talking about the tournament that takes place over three days. There's an entry fee of ten tetrals."

"Oh, no," said the clerk. "For that tournament, you have to be a war mage."

"I am a war mage." She reached into her shirt and pulled out her topaz on its steel chain.

The clerk stared, and his expression turned. He looked like a man who'd bitten into sour fruit.

Nalica leaned her six-foot longbow against her boot, stepped through, and bent the top half to effortlessly string it. "You need another demonstration?"

"No." The clerk leaned forward and lowered his voice. "Miss, there's something you don't understand about this tournament. The prize is a position as an officer in the city guard."

"I know. That's why I'm entering."

He looked at her as if she'd sprouted an extra head. "But you're a woman. You can't be in the city guard."

"Of course I can," said Nalica. "I used to lead a mercenary troop."

His nose wrinkled. "While that may be customary in the rural provinces, we do things differently in the imperial city."

Three gods. She'd come all the way to Riat and taken an overpriced room at the inn. There was no way she was letting this snooty clerk shut her out of the tournament. "The rules say nothing about the entrant having to be a man, only that the entrant be a war mage. Which I am."

"Yes, but...some things don't need to be said. They're implied."

"I didn't think it was implied that only men could enter," said Nalica. "Nor did the archer who showed me the way here. He seemed to think it was quite ordinary I should participate." She would not mention that the archer in question had also been eastern, from one of those rural provinces the clerk sneered at.

A man strolled in the door, dressed in the uniform of the Riat City Guard. His epaulettes indicated he was an officer. "Almost finished, Kaden?"

"Nearly," said the clerk. "I'm just running this woman off."

He turned and looked at Nalica. "Running her off, why?"

"She's trying to sign up for the archery tournament."

"Is she a war mage?"

"I am, sir," said Nalica, annoyed at being talked about as if she weren't there.

The officer turned to her. "Show me the stone."

She showed him the topaz.

The officer examined it and nodded. "Let her compete," he said to the clerk. "You know it won't make any difference. Meet me outside when you're done." He strolled out of the tent.

The infuriated clerk broke two pen nibs filling out her paperwork.

2 Vagabond's Day

The first day of the Triferian was Vagabond's Day, and it was the favorite of most Kjallans because it involved free whiskey. Nalica would not be able to indulge as much as she'd like to, not when she had the first round of the tournament that evening. She could afford to be neither drunk nor hung over, but a single drink in the morning would be fine. She'd brought her mug along for the purpose. At the first whiskey stand she came to, she filled it.

The merchants' tents had been erected and were now in service. In honor of the Vagabond, they'd been hung with blue streamers. Guards with the Riat insignia on their uniforms stood everywhere. Vagabond's Day, normally celebrated with whiskey and games of chance, had a tendency to become unruly. In the east, that often meant clan brawls. But here in Riat, it appeared the officials meant to keep order.

She angled away from the merchants' tents and passed by the fields where the games were held. All of them cost money to play, and she did not want to be tempted to spend her remaining quintetrals. Ahead was the racetrack. That seemed a safe place to wait out the day.

The festivalgoers at the rail were pressed up close, occupying nearly every bit of available space. Perhaps a race was in the offing. But when she found a gap at the rail and worked her way into it, she saw only an empty track. "What are we watching?" she asked the woman next to her.

"Vagabond's Dart is running," said the woman.

"That's a horse?"

The woman gave her a look. "He won the Plate last year, and the year before."

"Oh. So there's to be a race?"

"Not now," said the woman. "He's being exercised."

Nalica shrugged. Some fancy racehorse running on the track all by himself—sounded boring. She looked around and spotted a knot of archers gathered up at the rail not far away, the same men she'd seen yesterday evening. Caellus was there, ugh. But so was Justien, and she liked him, even if he did think he was going to beat her in the tournament.

She left her spot and went to the archers, sidling alongside Justien. He raised his whiskey mug when he saw her. "Great One, pass us by," he intoned.

She repeated the prayer, and they each took a swallow.

"I hope you're in top form tonight," she said.

He smiled. "You'd better not hope for that. You know the first round is no magic?"

"I savvy it."

"Well, then." He shrugged and returned his gaze to the track.

"Are you here to watch Vagabond's Dart?" she asked.

"It beats playing Knots or Knucklebones," said Justien.

"I'd rather watch a real race," said Nalica. "Not just one horse running around the track for exercise."

"It's no ordinary horse," said Caellus, from the other side of Justien. "Vagabond's Dart has won the Imperial Plate two years running. He's about to make it three."

"I hear he can't outrun Honeycatcher," said Justien.

"I've heard that too," said Caellus. "And I don't believe it."

"We'll see tomorrow night," said Justien.

"Who's Honeycatcher?" asked Nalica.

"New horse," said Justien. "Chestnut stallion, imported from Sardos. Supposed to be a great runner, but I've never seen him in a race."

"Dart hasn't been running well lately," put in a man on the rail near Nalica.

"I hope Honeycatcher wins," said Nalica, for no particular reason except that it seemed excessive for one horse to win the same prize three years in a row.

"You shouldn't," said Caellus. "Vagabond's Dart is owned by the captain of the Riat City Guard."

"He is?" The captain of the Riat City Guard would be her boss if she won the tournament. Not if. *When* she won the tournament.

Cheers went up from the crowd across the way, and she turned to watch the track. A horse sprinted around the far side, to the oohs and aahs of the spectators. The animal was a dark bay, almost black, with a white sock on his right hind.

"The captain of the guard does not *own* Vagabond's Dart," said Justien. "He owns a piece of him."

Nalica blinked. "How can someone own a piece of a horse?"

"Which piece?" asked another archer.

"The captain is part of a syndicate," said Justien. "He's one of seven people who own the horse jointly. Captain Felix pays a seventh of the horse's expenses, and he receives a seventh of his earnings."

"Oh." She'd never heard of that, horses being owned by groups of people. She supposed it was not dissimilar from clan ownership of herds.

The horse flew past, its churning hooves spitting dust clods over the track.

Justien turned to her. "Excitement's over. You progged? Want to get something to eat?"

She smiled—he still knew his eastern words, even if he only used them with her. In fact she was hungry, but festival food was more expensive than what she could find in the city. Her money wouldn't last if she spent it imprudently. "Well," she hedged, "I wasn't planning on eating at the festival."

"Come on now, I'll buy," said Justien. "We've already got the whiskey."

The whole situation was awkward. This man wasn't her friend; he was her competitor. He might feel generous toward her now, since he didn't think she had a chance of winning. But when evening rolled around and he saw how well she could shoot, she had a feeling he might regret his earlier kindness.

"I insist," said Justien.

"All right." He was the only man from eastern Kjall she'd met since leaving home. It made sense that she should at least pick his brain about how to get by as an easterner in the south.

He smiled and took her hand to lead her away from the rail.

She walked beside him through the festival grounds, aware of his big hand holding hers, of his body heat and his sheer size beside her. She'd been away from home a year now, and even compared to her family members she was tall. She was not accustomed to being towered over.

He stopped at two tents in succession, buying first two bags of roasted chestnuts and then some grilled meat and vegetables on sticks. They found seats in a deserted corner of the racetrack viewing area.

"I know you're eastern," said Justien, settling his huge body onto the too-small seat. "Am I right in guessing you're from the Vereth highlands?"

"Exactly right. And you?"

"Born and raised, but haven't been back in years," said Justien. "What clan are you from? Please don't say Kelden."

Nalica almost choked on the grilled pepper she was eating. She *was* from Clan Kelden. "You must be from Clan Polini."

"I am. So you are Kelden, then." He shook his head. "I should have known."

"I suppose we're enemies," said Nalica.

Justien's chewing slowed. "If it doesn't bother you, it doesn't bother me. Hardly seems to matter anymore."

He was right; the old feuds seemed so far away. When she'd been a girl, the battles between neighboring clans had meant something. Her family had land and herds to protect. Now that land—well, it wasn't worthless, but you couldn't do much more than herd goats and cattle on it, and the farmers in the lowlands were producing better animals. These days hardly anyone in the mountains could turn a profit from herding. Most of her people had sold off their stock. "It doesn't bother me."

"You have the tattoo?"

She nodded, opening her right fist to show him. The Kelden half-moon was on the palm of her hand. It was why she kept her hands closed most of the time, or at her sides with palms turned toward her thighs. Southern Kjallans didn't wear clan marks.

He set down his food and took her hand to examine it. "That's the Kelden mark, all right." He traced the tattoo with his fingers.

It tickled, but she held her hand still, not wanting him to let go.

"You'll be Yvar's get," he said.

She nodded. "Yvar is my father."

"Thought so." He grimaced.

She swallowed. "Let's see yours." She took his right hand and flipped it over. There it was, the Polini double hash mark. As he had done, she ran her fingers along the black markings. She knew what Justien was probably thinking, if he could put the clan differences behind him. He hoped to seduce her, to find himself a bedmate for the duration of the festival. And she, in her foolishness, was encouraging him. She'd sleep with him in a heartbeat except that after this evening they'd be enemies, and not because of any clan marks.

"Have you guessed my father's name?" asked Justien.

"Lerran," said Nalica.

"Right you are."

It was a funny thing. A decade ago, if Justien and Nalica, the son and daughter of rival clan lords, had been caught together, it would have been scandalous. But nobody cared anymore. The clans had scattered to the winds. Yvar was an old man, crippled by joint pain, and Lerran was dead.

"Tell me your history," said Justien. "How did you become a war mage?"

"My father had no sons," said Nalica. "We had the riftstone, which had been my grandfather's. When Yvar came to understand that there would be no male issue, he talked of selling it. We'd sold off most of our stock years ago, and money was tight."

Justien nodded. "My clan sold its stock, too."

"My mother convinced him to give the topaz to me instead," said Nalica. "She said it was my right to have it, since I was his heir. We barely had the money to pay for my training—in fact I'm pretty sure my mother borrowed most of it. I hope to pay her back someday."

"So you became a war mage."

"The idea was that if I had war magic, I'd always be able to find work, even if the clan fell apart. Which it did." How ironic, that her family had once believed a war mage would always be employable.

"What have you done since then?" Justien asked.

"After we sold off the herds, my father organized what was left of the clan into a mercenary troop. We hired on to guard unpopular lords, escort caravans, sometimes fight on one side or the other of a skirmish."

His brows rose. "You became a mercenary."

She nodded. "For the last several years, since Yvar was too infirm, I've been the leader of the troop. But there's not enough work for mercenaries anymore. The emperor has thrown out the unpopular lords, and he sends his battalions in to quiet the skirmishes. We're simply not needed the way we used to be. And there's not enough money in guarding caravans."

"You're right about that," said Justien, rolling his eyes.

"What about you? You left earlier than I."

Justien nodded. "Around the time we sold off the stock. My father died in a duel. It wasn't with anyone of your clan."

"I heard about it." Her family had celebrated when they'd heard the news, but now she felt a little embarrassed about that.

"All our best people were leaving to look for work. My mother had no money, and she had my younger brother and sister to support. So I trained at the palaestra and joined the imperial army as a prefect. The pay was steady, and I sent my salary home. When the emperor disbanded Red Eagle battalion, I found myself out of work. I looked for another spot, but nothing was available. Since then I've scraped by the way you have: odd jobs, escorting caravans."

"You still send money home?"

"When I can."

Now she felt guilty. He needed the job as much as she did, arguably more so since he was supporting his extended family. She only needed to pay her own way and repay the debt to her mother.

No, she could not afford to think like this. She was more qualified; at least, she hoped the tournament would demonstrate that. She could not feel sympathy for Justien. He might have a family to support, but he was a man. He probably got ten times as many job offers as she did. And clearly he had more money, if he could afford to eat at the festival and she couldn't.

Why had she let him pay her way? To lead him on was absolute foolishness. She fished some quintetrals out of her coin pouch. "Here," she said, placing them on the seat next to him and standing. "Thank you for lunch."

He stared at the coins. "I said I was buying."

"I pay my own way."

His brow wrinkled, and his eyes lifted to meet hers. "Did I offend you?"

"No. Please...it's just..." She exhaled. "I don't think we should get involved. Considering the circumstances."

Justien spread his hands. "It's just lunch."

"I don't think we should talk to each other anymore." She turned and walked away.

"Archers, string your bows."

Justien bent the bow and strung it effortlessly, even without his war magic. An official had come in turn to each competitor to take away their riftstones. Justien hated being without his riftstone. It was unpleasant to be separated from what was literally a fragment of his soul trapped within the stone. But it would not unduly affect his performance. He was confident of his ability to shoot without magic.

Many war mages ceased to drill and practice after soulcasting, instead depending entirely on magic for their battlefield prowess. And that magic was substantial; to a large extent they could get away with it. Even so, Justien was not that sort of war mage. He kept his physical skills sharp.

He looked down the line of his competitors, some to his left and some to his right. Caellus was struggling to string his bow. Typical; he was one of the lazy ones. Another man, whom Justien had never met, couldn't string his at all. He would be eliminated. The others had all managed to string their bows, including Nalica three places from his right. Good for her. It didn't surprise him terribly; she looked strong, and he doubted she would put herself through a competition like this if she couldn't accomplish this basic task.

He wished he'd watched her string it.

To the left of the archery field was a short wooden fence, about the height of his waist, and behind it stood the spectators. The tournament had attracted several hundred festivalgoers. To the right of the field was a raised platform with seating for about twenty people. The three judges were up there, along with some officials responsible for administering the tournament. About half the seats on the platform were empty. It was rumored that the emperor and empress might observe the final round of the competition, and he guessed those empty seats were being held in reserve for them.

For this magic-free round of competition, they would shoot butts at one hundred yards. At home, he'd used wooden casks for the purpose, but in southern Kjall, the butts were mounds of grass-covered earth, each about seven feet tall and four feet wide. A soft wooden staff about two inches wide leaned against the front of each butt. This was called the wand. The archer's goal was to split the wand, which required both power and incredible accuracy. If the arrow struck the butt, it was a hit; if it missed entirely, it was a sin. But if the archer split the wand, that earned the most points of all.

"Archers ready," called an official from the platform.

Justien nocked his first arrow. He raised his arm as he drew back the string, engaging his back and shoulder muscles. He was right-eye dominant. When shooting, he faced to the right, toward the judges' platform. The crowd had fallen silent. He narrowed the focus of his senses. There was nobody here at all, nobody but him and his bow and the wand, one hundred yards away.

"Loose," called the official.

Justien double-checked his position. He adjusted his draw a tiny bit and loosed the arrow. The crowd cheered.

He had a hit! His arrow had landed on the butt, a little high and a little to the right of the wand. He'd correct for that and get it eventually.

How had his competitors done? Caellus had a hit too—he was in better form than usual. Perhaps he'd practiced. Nalica's arrow was on the butt too, a bit low. Of the other competitors, roughly half had hits and the rest of them sins.

Nalica appeared to be left-eye dominant, since she was facing his direction, toward the crowd instead of the judges' stand. He caught her eye and smiled a silent congratulations.

She looked away without smiling back.

"Archers ready," called the official.

He slid another arrow from the stand, nocked it, and lifted his bow, tuning out the crowd and his competitors. The official called for them to loose, but Justien took an extra moment to fine-tune his aim.

A roar rose from the crowd. He hadn't loosed yet, and the unexpected noise nearly startled him into sending his arrow on a wild flight. He held his arrow in check and scanned the butts. Someone had split the wand. Who was it? There, he saw it: the wand impaled on the grassy surface, pinned by the arrow. It was truly split, with half of it dangling toward the ground. Had Nalica's arrow done that? That was her target.

He glanced at Nalica and saw her raising a triumphant fist in the air.

Fierce anger stole over him. She'd made a lucky shot, nothing more. She was strong, and she had good form, but he would not let her steal this tournament from him.

The crowd fell silent, and he realized he was the only archer who hadn't loosed. Now, unfortunately, he was nervous. He aimed carefully and checked his form. Body turned just right, good stance, hand pulled back to his cheek, fingers relaxed.

He loosed the arrow and watched its flight. It landed on the butt, a little low.

The crowd applauded politely.

Suppressing a scowl, he turned away from Nalica, who surely taunted him with her eyes, and pulled the next arrow from the stand. They had six to shoot in all. He would split the wand this time. He'd split it twice to make sure he beat her.

His third arrow didn't split the wand, but landed right next to it. A little closer each time—he'd get there. He glanced at Nalica's target and saw that her arrow had landed on the edge of the butt. She'd nearly missed. The other competitors didn't worry him. Caellus was shooting better than usual and had all three arrows on the butt. Everyone else had at least one sin. Caellus had a good day once in a while, but Justien knew he couldn't sustain it over three days of competition.

Nalica, on the other hand, appeared to be a serious threat. He couldn't let her beat him, not with that city guard job on the line. He took up his next arrow and prepared to put it down the middle of the wand.

"Loose."

He loosed. He watched his arrow's flight, and when it sliced through the wand, sending a broken shard of wood spinning through the air, he leapt up with a shout of triumph. The crowd roared their approval. He'd done it!

He turned to see how Nalica had fared this time. She'd only just loosed her arrow. He followed its flight and watched in horror as it buried itself in the fresh wand the officials had laid upon her target. The crowd cheered louder than ever. Two competitors had split the wand in a single round—this was unprecedented.

Justien frowned. He was not at all happy to be sharing the honor, especially since this was Nalica's second wand in the competition, and only his first. What use was splitting the wand if his competitor did the same? She was still ahead of him in points.

"Archers ready."

Justien's final two shots were disappointing, both hits but nowhere near the wand. Nalica had flustered him.

Fortunately, Nalica did not split the wand a third time, but, like him, she landed her final two shots, and with four hits and two wands, she'd won the round. Justien was in second place with five hits and one wand, and Caellus was in third with six hits.

The crowd cheered. Justien knew most of the cheers were for Nalica. He'd split the wand, but she'd done it twice. In the spectators' eyes, that made her twice as good.

There was no awards ceremony, since this was only the first round of competition. The crowd drifted away to seek other entertainments. The official who'd taken their riftstones returned and handed the stones back to the competitors. Though the stones looked similar, each war mage could easily pick out his own. A mage of any kind could sense his riftstone through the fragment of his soul that was embedded in it. As the competitors draped their riftstones around their necks, the captain of the city guard, Felix Hadrianus, came forward to congratulate them. He spoke first with Caellus. Then he came to Justien and clasped his wrist. "Excellent shooting."

"Thank you, sir," said Justien, inclining his head. If he won the competition, he'd be working for this man.

"And with no magic," added Felix. "I can see you'd be a fine addition to the guard."

"I hope to prove that to you," said Justien.

The captain moved on to Nalica. "What a show you gave us! That was a piece of luck, splitting the wand twice."

Justien watched her out of the corner of his eye. If she'd split the wand once, that might have been luck. But twice?

That was skill. Would she dare correct the captain, given that he was judging the contest?

"Thank you, sir," she said.

Apparently she wouldn't. Well, he wouldn't have done it either. But that had to rankle, having her feat of skill attributed to luck. He waited to hear the captain say she'd be a fine addition to the guard, but after clasping her wrist, he simply walked away.

In response, she looked almost impassive, but a tiny line appeared in her forehead, an indication of worry perhaps, or hurt feelings.

His resentment faded, and he began to feel a little sorry for her. It must be hard being a woman and a war mage, and having even her extraordinary accomplishments minimized. But pity was a luxury he could not afford. He needed this job, and he was going to have to shoot better tomorrow and the next day. Her problems were her own to solve, and he had a family to support.

"That was good shooting," said Caellus as he passed, clapping Justien on the shoulder. "Too bad you couldn't outperform the girl."

"I'll grant that you were less terrible than usual," said Justien.

Caellus snorted and strode off with his bow on his back.

Justien met Nalica's eyes. It was considered good form to congratulate one's opponent, but envy choked his throat. He managed a curt nod in her direction and walked away.

Sage's Day

It was lonely being a woman and a war mage. Nalica had enjoyed her triumph last night, but she'd been the only one to celebrate it. Justien, on the other hand, seemed to have an easy camaraderie with the other archers. She envied that, knowing it was something she'd likely never possess. She tried to make friends, but most men simply didn't accept her. They fell into two categories: those who avoided her because they didn't know how to act around a woman like her, and those who actively harassed her.

And then there was Justien. He didn't seem to belong in either of those categories. But after her win last night, he wouldn't be friendly anymore. He'd liked her when he'd thought she wasn't serious competition. Now he knew better.

Never mind; she wasn't here for companionship. She was here to win that city guard job. She *had* to get that job. It might not mean acceptance from her peers, but it would at least mean a permanent position and a steady income. She could pay her mother back. And if she could stay in one place for a while, perhaps she might eventually make some friends who didn't think it was strange for a woman to be a war mage.

It was early morning on Sage's Day. The blue streamers for Vagabond's Day had been taken down and replaced with white ones for the Sage. The merchants' tents and food tents remained as they had been, but the whiskey stands had disappeared. The gaming area had been broken down and rebuilt to host a Caturanga tournament, some sort of musical competition, and a pyrotechnic exhibition.

The most important event of Sage's Day, at least for the typical festival attendee, was the Absolution. An enormous statue of the Sage had been erected in the center of the festival grounds, and stationed around it were dozens of small tents. If you had wronged somebody, you were to go into one of the tents, sprinkle yourself with consecrated water, and ask for the Sage's Absolution.

Nalica, who had never been particularly religious, avoided the Absolution. Instead, she browsed the merchants' tents, stopping at one to examine panes of colored window glass.

An electric sensation prickled on her neck. Turning, she saw Justien leaning against a post across the way. Despite the little frisson of excitement she felt at seeing him, she found herself disinterested in approaching. He had obviously resented her success in the tournament, since he hadn't congratulated her last night.

Ignoring him, she walked from the window glass tent to one exhibiting jewelry. The pieces were made from inexpensive stones and materials, but were artful nonetheless. Though she had no money to spend, she looked through the offerings.

Justien stepped up beside her. She considered walking away, but that felt like ceding him ground. If she wanted to examine jewelry, then pox it, she was going to examine jewelry.

Justien touched a necklace with a round blue stone. "This would look nice on you."

"It's not my color," said Nalica.

"Oh? Which one would you choose?"

After a moment's hesitation, she pointed to a necklace with a yellow stone.

"Ah, like your war mage's topaz." He caught the merchant's eye. "What type of stone is that?"

"Citrine," said the merchant. "A rare variety from Riorca. You rarely see color like that on this kind of stone. Try it."

Justien lifted the necklace from the table. "Let's see how it looks."

She shook her head. "I can't afford it." Maybe she could later, if she got the city guard job. But not now.

"We'll just look," said Justien.

He circled behind her, lifted her hair, and placed the necklace on her collarbone. Nalica swallowed. She barely noticed the necklace. His hand was on her neck, surprisingly gentle despite the man's strength and size.

He leaned around to see how the necklace looked from the front. "You're right. That is your color."

"I don't want it." She took the necklace off, placed it back on the table, and walked away.

He ran after her. "Please don't run off. I was rude last night. I apologize."

"You've nothing to apologize for." She hurried her steps, hoping that would discourage him.

"But I do—it was a sin of omission," said Justien. "I ought to have acknowledged your performance last night, but I missed the mark. So I'll do it now. Congratulations on your victory."

It was amazing how markedly a few words could affect her. Weak in the knees, she stopped walking and blinked rapidly to hold back the tears. The crowd had cheered for her last night, but her fellow archers hadn't been so enthusiastic. And neither had the captain of the guard, who'd attributed her two best shots to luck. It meant a lot to have a peer she respected express appreciation for her skill. "Thank you. And congratulations to you too."

"You shot better than I," said Justien. "I wish I'd said so last night. I'm afraid that at the time I was consumed with envy."

She snorted. "You don't envy me."

"I did last night," said Justien. "All of us did. I've never split the wand twice in a round."

Nalica had done it before many times in practice, but she would not say so. "You split it once, and you didn't have a single sin."

"If the competition were not so strong, that would have been enough," said Justien.

Nalica frowned. That was the crux of it, wasn't it? He acknowledged her ability, but he also resented it, because he didn't want to lose the tournament. "I suppose we cannot be friends," she said. "You want this job in the city guard, and so do I."

"I *need* that job," said Justien.

"So do I," said Nalica.

"May I make a suggestion?"

"What?" she asked warily. He'd better not ask her to throw the tournament so that he could win. She wouldn't let anyone take this prize from her.

"I know we both want the city guard job," said Justien. "We want it badly, and only one of us will have it. But we don't know yet who's going to win it, so let's be friends. I promise to congratulate you if you win. And if I win, you'll congratulate me. We'll be happy for one another whatever happens. What do you say?"

That sounded difficult, especially if he ended up being the winner. But it would be nice to have a friend, if only for a couple of days. She reached over and clasped his wrist. "That sounds fair."

He took her hand, and they strolled through the fairgrounds. Merchants barked their wares, but she paid them no mind. Her senses were full of Justien: his great presence by her side, the heat of his body, his callused hand in hers.

They'd come to the center of the festival grounds. Ahead loomed a painted bronze statue of the Sage in his robe, holding his familiar, a white fox. Guards in orange uniforms were all over the place. She counted over thirty of them, and they weren't the Riat City Guard. Several of them were women, which surprised and delighted her. Perhaps some were war mages.

"Justien." She nudged him. "Who are those guards?"

He turned in the direction she was looking and stiffened. "Oh—those are Legaciatti. Let's clear out." He took her arm and led her in the other direction.

"Legaciatti. You mean the emperor's personal guard?"

Justien nodded. "The emperor and empress perform an absolution at the Triferian every year. They must be here now, or perhaps they will be soon, and the guards are preparing the way for them."

She glanced back. "The emperor and empress are here at the festival?"

"Yes, they come every year for a few events. Best to stay away from their guards. We don't want trouble."

The tiny hope that had leapt within her at seeing an organization with women warriors in it faded now that she understood she could never join it. The Legaciatti were all orphans, recruited and trained for their roles from early childhood, to ensure their loyalty to the imperial throne. It would be nice if she could at least stay and talk with them.

But if they were on duty, and clearly they were, that wouldn't be permitted.

To avoid the crowd, she and Justien entered a covered stable of horses on exhibit, many of them for sale. They walked slowly, examining the horses' nameplates as they passed.

"Is it hard being a woman and a war mage?" Justien asked.

"Very hard," she blurted, and then regretted it. He didn't need to hear her whine about her problems.

"People treat you badly?"

She shrugged. "Not physically. Sometimes I get ugly comments. Mostly I'm just ignored. The mercenary troop accepted me, because they were my clan. They'd known me since I was little. But in southern Kjall it's different."

"*We're* different," said Justien. "Much as we try, we don't fit in here."

Nalica nodded. "I'm different twice over. Once for being a woman war mage, and again for being eastern. Back at home I had more suitors than I knew what to do with, but the men here don't find me appealing."

"They're fools," said Justien. "And I'll tell you something. Some of those southern women look so fragile I'd be afraid of breaking them."

Nalica smiled and glanced at him sidelong. "I don't break easily."

He looked at her intently, and she knew that the two of them were thinking the same thing. Could they have a festival romance? Would it affect their performances tonight and the night after? What would happen at the end of the tournament, when one of them won and the other didn't?

While many easterners took a dim view of casual romances, southern Kjallans did not. Brief affairs were common here among unmarried men and women, and she'd indulged in a couple of them herself. But this was different. She and Justien were competitors. No matter what, this was going to end badly.

"Halt." A guard stepped away from the wall and blocked their path. "This is a restricted area."

Nalica stopped. "I thought these horses were on exhibit."

"*Those* horses are on exhibit." The guard waved at the aisle they'd just come down. "*These* are not." He waved at the ones in the aisle they were about to enter. "These are the horses racing tomorrow."

"Oh, you mean like Honeycatcher and Vagabond's Dart." She stretched up to see over the guard's shoulder. The stalls weren't all full; in fact most were empty. There appeared to be three empty stalls between each horse. She spotted a dark head peering over the stall door. "Is that Vagabond's Dart?"

"He's in the other building," said the guard.

"Hey," called a man from just down the aisle. "Aren't you the archers from the tournament last night?"

Nalica took one look at him and thought, *money*. He was well groomed and dressed in a fine silk syrtos.

The newcomer approached the guard and said, "Leave them be, Tullian. These are the competitors from last night. One of them will be joining your number soon."

As Tullian moved aside, Nalica noticed the Riat City Guard emblem on his shoulder.

"My name is Philo," said the well-dressed man. "You two shot very well."

"Thank you," said Nalica.

Justien echoed the sentiment.

"Were you here to see the racehorses?" asked Philo.

"We're just passing through," said Justien.

"I'll show you my horse if you'd like."

Nalica shrugged and then nodded. Why not?

Philo led them nine stalls down the aisle to a chestnut who poked his head over the stall door. "This is Honeycatcher."

"Oh," said Justien, sounding impressed. "You own Honeycatcher?"

"Indeed. Imported him from Sardos." Philo stroked the animal's nose. "You can pet him if you like. He's kind."

As Nalica reached for the chestnut's nose, the horse pushed its head into her hands. She stroked his bony face and soft muzzle. Justien's hand reached up beside hers and did the same.

"He's delightful," said Nalica.

The owner beamed. "I've never seen a stallion with such a fine temperament. He loves people, and he loves to run."

"Is he going to win tomorrow?" asked Justien.

"Absolutely," said the owner. "He's faster than Dart. And he throws foals with kind temperaments."

"Dart's reputed to be nasty," said Justien.

"Bites and kicks, yes," said the owner. "I don't care how fast he is, no good can come of breeding a vicious horse. Top riders can handle him, sure. But what about the foals he sires who don't become racehorses? They've got to get along with people."

"Well, I hope Honeycatcher wins." Nalica wasn't an experienced horsewoman, and because of that she sympathized with what the man was saying. She'd had to ride ill-mannered, uncooperative horses on more than one occasion, and those were not experiences she wanted to repeat.

"He will," said the owner. "And one of you had better win tonight. I'll be watching."

She and Justien thanked him.

Nalica could see daylight at the other end of the stable, and the guard who'd stopped them before was now leaning against the wall, looking disinterested. They could go out this way and save themselves a long walk back along the aisle.

Justien took her hand and led her in that direction, past the remaining racehorses. "The run for the Imperial Plate is this evening, after the tournament," he said. "Want to watch it with me? The emperor and empress will be there."

The emperor and empress of Kjall—that would be a sight. But she probably shouldn't spend more time with Justien. Who knew how they'd feel about each other after the second round of competition? And especially the third. "I'll think about it."

A man came out of the tack room just ahead. Justien and Nalica veered to avoid him. Then Justien stopped suddenly and held out his arm. "Captain Felix."

The man blinked as if startled. He clasped wrists with Justien, but the look on his face was blank and uncomprehending.

"I'm from the archery tournament," prompted Justien.

The captain's face lit in recognition, and he relaxed. "Oh, right." He nodded at Nalica. "Justien and Nalica, two of our best archers in the competition. You're going to give us a good show tonight, I hope."

"Sir, I'll be winning tonight's round," said Justien.

"So he believes," said Nalica.

The captain grinned. "I love to see that competitive spirit."

He walked away, and they continued on their path out of the stable. The encounter with the captain had broken the spell between them, and Nalica decided she'd had enough of Justien's company. She needed to keep her mind off Justien and on the round of competition to come. She made her excuses and drifted away into the crowd.

Nalica strapped her arm guard into place, glancing nervously around her fellow competitors. It was the second round of the tournament, and after last night, she was in the lead. The prize was hers to lose.

It was five minutes until they loosed their first arrows. There were no early-round eliminations in this tournament, and all the competitors were present except Caellus. It astonished her that Caellus could be so cavalier about being on time. She'd arrived an hour early just in case.

Today they kept their riftstones and would be shooting with magic at a distance of two hundred yards. The butts looked ridiculously far away, but war mages could shoot from great distances. The magic did, however, have its limitations. At short range, Nalica could shoot arrows with perfect, magically enhanced accuracy. But this ability broke down at longer distances. During this round of competition, her war magic would grant her the sharpened vision she needed to see the target clearly and sufficient strength to send an arrow all that distance, but otherwise accuracy would be up to her.

Just as an official raised his bugle to signal the start of the second round, Caellus came running up, his bow jangling on his back. "Sorry," he said, quickly stringing it and nocking an arrow.

"Archers ready," called the official.

Nalica raised her bow, drew it with an upward motion of her arm, and aimed.

"Loose."

The arrow sang as she let it fly. She loved the music of this sport: the twang of the string, the whine of the arrow. She tracked her arrow visually, raising a hand to her forehead to block the sun. It landed on the butt, and she smiled. It hadn't split the wand, but no one was likely to do that at this distance.

She scanned her competitors' targets. Everyone was shooting well today. Caellus, Justien, and two others had also scored hits. The audience cheered—they were impressed simply by the distance.

Caellus drew a second arrow from the stand. He turned to Justien, who was shooting beside him. "You hear about Honeycatcher?"

"Hear what?" asked Justien.

"He's been pulled from tonight's race," said Caellus.

"Whatever for?" Justien tested the string of his bow and nocked a second arrow.

"Not fit to run."

Nalica turned toward them. "But he was fine when we saw him this morning."

"You saw him?" Caellus looked skeptical.

"In the stable," said Justien.

"Archers ready," called the official. "Loose."

Nalica's second arrow went wild and didn't hit the butt at all. She cursed under her breath. Caellus's didn't land either, but Justien's did. Pox it all, that put him in the lead.

What had happened to Honeycatcher? It seemed quite a coincidence that he should become ill right before his big race. The illness must have come on quickly, because the horse had looked fine when she and Justien had seen him. Could someone have poisoned or otherwise sickened the horse? She and Justien had gotten past the guard; surely other people could have done the same if they'd tried.

Captain Felix of the city guard had been inside the stable. She glanced up at the platform, where he sat watching the competition as one of its three judges. What had he been doing in the tack room just hours before Honeycatcher, a rival to his own horse, fell ill? Might he be under suspicion for his presence there? Come to think of it, she and Justien might be under suspicion themselves.

"Loose."

She readied herself and loosed her third arrow. Right onto the butt, as was Justien's. Caellus had scored a hit, too. It rankled to be tied with Caellus; she knew she was better.

She caught Justien's eye with a worried look, wondering what he thought about the horse. He simply smiled at her. She managed to smile back. It appeared he wasn't thinking about the horse at all. Well, fair enough; it wasn't his business, nor was it hers. She'd follow his example and forget about it, at least for now.

She landed her last two arrows on the butts, but the damage was done. She had five hits and one sin. Justien had six hits, no sins. Caellus had four hits, two sins, which meant that Justien had won this round, and she'd come in second.

How did she sit in the overall standings? She'd won yesterday and Justien had won today. But she'd won yesterday by a greater margin because, in most tournaments, splitting the wand was worth a lot more than scoring a hit. She might still be in first place. Regardless, it all came down to her performance tomorrow.

She'd made a deal with Justien that she would congratulate him if he won, so she walked up to him and held out her hand. "Nice shooting. Congratulations."

He clasped her wrist and smiled warmly. "Nice shooting yourself."

Well, that hadn't been too excruciating. She turned to go.

"Wait," called Justien. "You want to watch the Imperial Plate with me?"

"The horse race?" She'd forgotten that he'd invited her earlier.

"I know Honeycatcher isn't running anymore, but I'm sure it will be exciting. And you could see the imperial family."

The other archers began to bleed away into the crowd. She was flattered by Justien's invitation, but if she stayed for the race, she wouldn't have time to return to town for a meal, and she couldn't afford to eat on the festival grounds again. She leaned in and spoke in a low voice. "I need to run back to the inn for supper. But I'd like to talk to you after the race. Could we meet this evening in a place where there aren't so many people?"

"I could meet you at the inn in town. Where are you staying?"

"The Crooked Billet."

His brow wrinkled in thought. "That's on the west side?"

"It's far, I know," said Nalica. "Why don't I meet you back here at the fairgrounds. Say, by the registration tent in a few hours."

He nodded. "I'll see you then."

Justien had been waiting by the registration tent for thirty minutes in the dark, and Nalica had yet to show up. She hadn't told him what she wanted to speak to him about. He hoped it wasn't about the tournament, because that subject would be awkward. He'd outshot her tonight. He'd proven that he could beat her. If he could repeat that performance tomorrow, he would win the city guard job—and if she thought she could talk him out of that, she could think again.

He'd watched the horses run for the Imperial Plate. It had, unfortunately, been a snoozer of a race. Vagabond's Dart had broken fast and led the pack to the first turn. From there, he'd gradually lengthened his lead and ultimately crossed the finish line alone. Captain Felix would be happy, at least. The purse was five thousand tetrals, and if Justien understood the arrangement correctly, Felix would receive one-seventh of it.

A figure detached itself from the crowd and moved toward him. It was Nalica—had to be. He couldn't see well in this unlit section of the festival grounds, but her size and shape were unmistakable.

"Sorry if I'm late," she said as she came up to him. "It's a long walk from town."

"You should just eat at the festival next time," he said, and immediately regretted the words. If she wasn't eating at the festival, she had a reason for that, and the reason was probably that she was short on tetrals.

"That would be more convenient," she said blandly. "Look, about the horse—"

"What horse?"

"Honeycatcher," she said. "You and I saw him this morning. He looked fine. So why was he scratched from the race?"

Justien shrugged, feeling oddly defensive about this subject. It had shaken him to bump into the captain of the guard near Honeycatcher's stall. "How should I know? He's a racehorse. They go lame; they get sick."

"And Captain Felix was there, coming out of the tack room," said Nalica, "when his horse was stabled in the other barn. Don't you think it's odd that he was there? What was he doing?"

"He didn't poison the horse, if that's what you're thinking." He could not imagine the captain of the guard doing such a thing. At least, he didn't want to imagine it.

Nalica raised her brows. "Are you certain he didn't?"

Justien was about to spit out a reflexive *yes*, but out of respect he paused to think the situation over. "I cannot be certain, but I see no reason to accuse him. All we saw him do was walk out of a tack room. That's not a crime."

"I'm not saying it's a crime," said Nalica. "I'm just saying that maybe we're the only people who know he was there, and maybe we should tell someone about it."

Justien bit his lip. If they did, there might be an investigation. Given the captain's position of authority, it was hard to say whether he'd be hauled in for questioning or not. But he could easily find out that Justien and Nalica had been the ones to report him, and he was one of the contest judges. "Perhaps we could say something after the tournament."

"I think we should speak up sooner rather than later," said Nalica.

"I don't think a crime was committed," said Justien. "I think it was just bad luck. The animal got sick at an inconvenient time."

"You're probably right," said Nalica. "But in case you're not, shouldn't we pass on what we know to the appropriate people? To the horse's owner, if no one else. He seemed like a nice man."

Justien sighed. "I really don't want to get involved in this."

Her brows rose. "Why, are you afraid?"

He frowned. Yes, he was afraid. What if this got in the way of his winning the city guard job? Or even if it didn't, what if it ruined his relationship with Captain Felix, the man who might become his boss? All because of some "evidence" he'd taken to the authorities that was trivial and not even incriminating. And those weren't even the worst of the possible consequences. He and Nalica had been at the stables too. What if suspicion fell upon them?

"It would be better if we went together," said Nalica. "But if you won't talk, I'll do it on my own."

"No, you won't."

"You can't stop me."

Now he was getting angry. Did this woman not know when to mind her own business? If she got involved, any number of bad things could happen, not just to Captain Felix or to Justien, but to Nalica herself. He and Nalica were easterners, and they'd been seen in the stable only hours before the horse had sickened. Nalica hadn't been in the south long enough to understand that foreigners in Riat were often regarded with mistrust. If someone needed a scapegoat, they would look no further than Justien or Nalica.

He took her arm and pulled her close. "I want you to keep your nose out of places it doesn't belong," he hissed into her ear. "Have you considered the possibility that suspicion might fall on us? We were in that stable, too."

"But we didn't do anything. A truth spell would confirm that."

"You're an easterner," he said. "You think they waste truth spells on people like us?"

Her brow wrinkled. "If you're saying the city guard is crooked, that's all the more reason we should tell someone about Captain Felix."

"I'm not saying that."

"Then I don't understand you," she said. "Shouldn't we help the man whose horse might have been poisoned?"

"You have *no idea* if that happened," he said fiercely. "*No idea.*"

"I just want—" She looked up into his eyes, and something changed in her face. "Never mind." She pulled out of his grasp and walked away.

Soldier's Day

The next morning, Nalica was back at the fair for Soldier's Day. The white streamers had been replaced with orange ones, and the local battalion had been turned out. They marched in formation in the central square and performed demonstration drills. A field on the east side of the grounds had been given over to athletic games: foot races, jumping contests, and throwing contests.

She tried to work up the courage to speak to the authorities about what she'd seen in the stable yesterday, but Justien had instilled in her a little apprehension. He did know southern Kjall better than she did. Perhaps he was right. If she stuck her nose where it didn't belong, suspicion might easily fall upon her—and upon him, since they'd been together at the time.

On the other hand, the horse's owner, Philo, already knew who they were. He'd recognized them as archery competitors, so if he suspected them, he would surely approach them at the tournament tonight, or have the guards do so.

Uncertain what to do, she wandered the festival grounds almost at random until she discovered, to her delight, an informal archery competition for novices, with small, weak bows provided. This must be the one the clerk had mentioned. She smiled at the sight of the arrows, so short compared to the thirty-inch ones that fit her longbow. She found a seat and watched the competitors, mostly children, struggle with the coordination of handling bow, string, and arrow.

She'd been sitting there over an hour when Justien strode up. "I've looked everywhere for you. Can we go someplace quiet to talk?"

She nodded and let him lead her away.

When they'd reached a quiet corner of the festival grounds, Justien said, "I've changed my mind. Let's talk to the authorities."

She blinked. That was the last thing she'd expected him to say. "Really?"

"Right now," he said. "Let's go together."

"Why'd you change your mind?"

He shrugged. "I don't know. It's been nagging at me, that's all."

"Who do you think we should tell?"

He made a face. "I would say the city guard, but Felix is their captain. No one's going to investigate his own boss."

"Who else, then? Philo?"

Justien nodded. "I think he's our best option. I don't know anything about him, but he must be wealthy and connected if he can import a fancy racehorse from Sardos. Maybe he'll know what to do with the information."

"If anyone cares about what happened to Honeycatcher, it's the man who owns him," said Nalica.

They headed to the stable and down the aisle where the racehorses were kept. A guard, not the same one as before, stepped up to block them as they approached the racehorse stalls. "Off limits."

Nalica peered around him at Honeycatcher's distant stall. The horse was still there, poking his nose over the door. The owner was present too, sitting on a chair in front of the stall and looking over a handful of papers.

"Philo. Sir!" called Nalica past the guard. "Can we speak to you for a moment?"

"He's not ready to be moved yet," said Philo without looking up.

"We want to talk to you," said Nalica. "About the reason Honeycatcher isn't feeling well."

That got his attention. As he turned toward them, recognition lit his eyes. He got up and approached, looking much less friendly than the day before. "You know something about that?"

Nalica took a second look at the guard. The insignia showed he was one of Felix's men. "Can we speak privately?"

With a sniff of exasperation, Philo motioned them away from the guard and the racehorses. When they were sufficiently distant, he halted. "Tell me what you know."

"It's really not much," admitted Nalica. "Only that when we were here yesterday, we saw Captain Felix coming out of the tack room."

"Who's this Felix?"

"Captain of the Riat City Guard," said Justien. "Part-owner of Vagabond's Dart."

"I'll tell you who else was here yesterday," said Philo. "You two."

"Well...yes," said Nalica. "We said that already."

"Honeycatcher was poisoned," said Philo. "And I intend to find out who did it."

"It wasn't us," said Justien.

"I didn't see where you went after I showed you Honeycatcher," said Philo. "You might have gone into the tack room yourself. You might have gone into the feed room."

"If we'd done it, why would we come here?"

"That's a good question." Philo folded his arms. "I'd like to hear the answer. After we get a mind mage here who can administer a truth spell."

"If you want me to submit to a truth spell to convince you I'm innocent, I'll do it," said Nalica.

"So will I," said Justien.

Philo's expression softened. "Well...I don't think I can get a mind mage here on short notice. I'll be talking to the authorities, though. If I need that truth spell from you, I'll get it."

"We're in the archery tournament tonight," said Justien. "You know where to find us."

Philo's brow wrinkled. "Did you see Captain Felix do anything he shouldn't have, while he was here?"

Justien shook his head. "Nothing at all. We just wanted you to know we saw him in the area."

"Go on, then," said Philo. "I'll fetch you if you're needed."

As they left the stable, Justien let out a sigh. "I'm glad that's over. It was bothering me. You know what I mean?"

"I know exactly what you mean," said Nalica. It was out of their hands now. Maybe they'd done somebody a bit of good and maybe they hadn't, but at least they'd tried to do the right thing. She didn't fear the possibility of a truth spell, as long as it was administered fairly.

"What are your plans for the rest of the day?" asked Justien.

Nalica hesitated, distracted by the sight of a man in a plain brown syrtos who browsed the wares of a knife vendor. In a low voice, she said to Justien, "That man at the knife tent—do you know him?"

"Never seen him before in my life," rumbled Justien.

"I have. I saw him at the kids' archery tournament, around the time you showed up. Then I saw him again before we went into the stable. And here he is a third time."

"It's a festival," said Justien. "He can go where he wants. What, you think he's following us?"

"Walk with me and let's find out." She took his hand and led him away, taking no particular care which direction she went. They walked down an aisle of merchant tents selling clothes and belts and boots, and then turned in to an aisle with food vendors.

"Something smells good," said Justien. "I'm progged. How about you?"

Nalica glanced backward. The man was there. He hadn't yet made the turn down their aisle but was examining a pair of boots at the cobbler's tent. The hair went up on the back of her neck.

"Look behind us," she said quietly to Justien. "Don't be too obvious about it. He's there."

Justien turned and looked. "I'll be poxed. So he is."

"Don't *stare*," she hissed.

"I'm going to poxing look right at him," said Justien. "He wants to say something to us, he can come up and say it."

"What if it's something to do with Honeycatcher?"

"Can't see why it would be. But let's ask him." Justien took her hand and led her back through the crowd, toward the man in the brown syrtos. But by the time they'd woven their way through the other festivalgoers to the cobbler's tent, the man was gone.

Nalica looked all over, but she didn't see him anywhere. "I think you scared him."

"Good," said Justien. "Aren't you progged? Let's have lunch."

"I can't." She was down to her last coins and at best could only afford a bit of bread and cheese, and that only in town, not at the festival.

He eyed her. "Can't or won't?"

She said nothing. If she admitted she was out of money, he might offer her some, and she didn't want charity. She didn't want to feel obligated toward him, not before the final round of a tournament in which they were essentially tied for first place.

"Are you out of money?" he asked softly.

Gods, why hadn't she thought of an excuse to be rid of him before now? "No."

"You don't have to pretend," said Justien. "I've been there. I've been dead broke many times since Red Eagle was disbanded."

"I'm not *dead broke*," she growled.

"Let me buy you lunch," said Justien. "No obligation, no expectations. My friends have bought for me many a time, and I buy for them when they're hard up. I'd hate to see you go into the third round of the tournament hungry."

"Why not?" said Nalica. "It would be to your benefit."

He grinned. "I'd rather beat you when you're in top form."

"I could beat you if I hadn't eaten in a week."

Justien took her hand and squeezed it. "Look, this isn't generosity on my part. I know we'll be parting ways after tonight. I'd like to get to know you a bit more before that happens."

"Isn't that a waste of time, under the circumstances?"

"How can it be, if I'm enjoying myself?" said Justien. "Come on, let me buy this time."

She pretended to agonize over his proposition, but in fact she'd made up her mind a while ago. "All right."

After Justien had purchased each of them a bread bowl filled with beef stew, he led Nalica away from the crowd. Once more he found seats near the racetrack. There wouldn't be any races until later in the afternoon, and the area was deserted. He wanted privacy.

"I have to tell you this, because I was afraid to tell anyone in my clan," said Nalica as she took her seat. "I admired your father."

He raised his head, surprised. "How did you even know my father?"

"I didn't, really. I saw him once at the Ismorian Games."

"The Ismorian Games? Gods, that would have been..." He paused for a moment to do the math. "That would have been seventeen years ago. Am I right? That's the only one we went to in my lifetime. Some years we didn't go because of clan disputes, and then—well, you know. The games went into decline." The stew maker had given him no spoon to eat with, so he pulled his knife from the sheath at his belt and speared a piece of meat.

"Seventeen years ago," said Nalica. "You're right." She followed his lead and pulled out her knife.

"How old are you?" he asked.

"Twenty-six. I was nine at the time of the Games."

"Nalica, we're almost the same age. I'm just a year older." He could hardly believe it. This woman was perfect for him: exactly his type physically, from the same background, and a war mage like himself—a damned good one, at that. She was from a rival clan, but that didn't bother him. If only they weren't competitors in the archery tournament. If he'd met her under any other circumstances...

"You must have been at the games too, but I don't recall seeing you," said Nalica.

He shrugged. "I looked rather different then." As he recalled, he'd been running around with a pack of Polini boys at that age, causing trouble. He'd settled down a lot since those days.

"Do you know what I liked about your father?" said Nalica. "His kindness to his children. He lifted them up on his lap. He looked them in the eye when he talked to them."

Justien's chest tightened with grief at this description of his long-dead sire. Lerran had his faults, but he had been an excellent father. "The children you saw. How old were they?"

"I hardly remember," said Nalica. "It was so long ago. I remember Lerran the most. The children were small— certainly younger than you would have been. A boy and a girl, perhaps."

He nodded. "That would have been my younger brother and sister."

"The ones you now support?"

"They're grown now. I still send money to my mother." He'd speared all the meat out of his soup, one chunk at a time. Now he turned to the sweet potatoes.

"I'd heard so many rumors about your family before the Games, you know," said Nalica. "You were cattle thieves, liars, murderers. So I was fascinated by your father. I watched him in secret, wanting to know what evil looked like. And I saw this man lifting up his children and speaking to them with love and respect, and I wondered how true those accusations could really be."

"Somewhat true, I imagine," said Justien. The behavior of his clan-mates had not been exemplary. "But never mind. Did your father not like children?"

She tried to hide her wince, but he wasn't fooled. He set aside his bread bowl, took her hand, and squeezed it.

"He had only me," said Nalica. "He wanted a boy. He waited and waited, and the boy never came. He had no use for a girl."

"He gave you the riftstone."

"My mother made him do that," said Nalica. "She was proud of me."

"Is she still alive?"

Nalica nodded.

"I'd like to meet her someday."

A shadow passed over Nalica's features, and he knew she was thinking what he was thinking. They had no future together after tonight.

"Look, I..." He trailed off, not certain what to say. He wanted her, but he also wanted that gods-cursed city guard job. "There was something I wanted to ask, only..." He was afraid to ask it. "Oh, pox it," he said finally. He leaned forward and kissed her.

She drew back just a little in surprise—or perhaps his beard had tickled her. But an instant later she was leaning in and kissing him back. He reached for her and wrapped a hand around the back of her neck, pulling her close.

She smelled of leather and yew and something floral he couldn't identify—something she bathed with, perhaps. Everything about her felt powerful: her lips, her frame, her arms as they reached around him to complete the embrace. Her hair, not yet braided for competition, was soft beneath his fingers. He wanted to know every inch of her.

Nalica pulled away. "Being with me won't bring any of it back. The clans, the herds. Your father."

"I know that." He stared, mesmerized, at her kiss-bitten lips.

"I've changed since those days."

"We all have," he said. "We change or we die."

Nalica turned, unable to meet his gaze. "I can't do this."

His heart sank. "Because of the tournament?"

"Because of the tournament."

"We should talk about that."

"There is nothing to say." Her eyes had gone distant. She had her game face on. "One of us will win tonight, and the other will leave town in search of another job."

"It doesn't have to be that way," said Justien.

"I see no alternative."

A moment ago he might have agreed with her. But now he saw a way forward—one that would please him in more ways than one. "Do you not?" he asked gently. When she did not respond, he continued. "A city guard's pay can support two people."

She looked at him warily. "What are you suggesting?"

His mouth felt suddenly dry, and he swallowed. "If I win tonight, you can stay with me."

Her face was expressionless. "As your mistress?"

"If you desire," he said. "Or you could be my wife."

For several seconds, she was completely silent. "Did you just propose marriage, Justien?"

He swallowed again. "Well, it's contingent on my winning tonight. I won't take a wife if I can't support her."

Her eyes narrowed. "And what if I win tonight? Do you come and live with me, and I support you?"

"You haven't offered."

"And if I did?"

He lowered his head. "I don't think I could do that. I need to work. It's...in my blood. I wouldn't know what to do with myself otherwise." Not to mention that he would spend all his time consumed with jealousy over her job, which he wanted for himself.

"Did it not occur to you that I might feel the same way?"

"It did," he admitted. "But I had to ask." She was still an easterner at heart, it seemed. It was common in southern Kjall for a woman to manage the household and children while the husband held a job, but in eastern Kjall most women worked alongside the men. "Nalica..." He raised his eyes to hers, which were a lovely hazel. "I think I fell in love the moment I laid eyes on you. Or perhaps it happened when you split the wand that first time."

She smiled.

"Regardless of how it happened, you're the woman I want. I know we only met two days ago, but I am certain of this, more certain than I've ever been of anything."

A line appeared in the middle of her forehead. He couldn't tell if she was alarmed by his words or pleased by them.

"And—how do you feel?" he stammered. "About me."

"I want you," she said, lowering her eyelids. "But it's not possible. You know it is not. Only one of us can win the tournament."

Yes, only one of them could win. And regardless of who did, he was going to walk away unsatisfied. Even if he got the job, he could not have the woman.

Back at the tournament site, Nalica laid the base of her bow against her boot and stepped through with her other foot, preparing to string the weapon. She paused as orange-garbed Legaciatti swarmed onto the field. Some of them took up positions among the spectators. Others placed themselves on the archery field, behind the competitors. She sniffed. What did they think she was going to do, loose an arrow at the emperor?

She checked to make sure the bottom of her bow was secure between her legs and bent the top half toward her to hook the bowstring. With the aid of her war magic, it was an easy task.

A clump of Legaciatti moved toward the judge's platform. She watched, guessing that the emperor and empress must be at the center of the clump. When they ascended the stairs, she caught a brief glimpse of the imperial couple. The emperor was known to be a cripple; he'd lost the lower half of his left leg in an assassination attempt years ago. Despite that, Nalica saw no limp in his stride. She'd heard he wore a false leg, which he seemed to get around quite well on.

The imperials reached the platform and took their seats, flanked by Legaciatti. Now she could see Emperor Lucien clearly. The emperor was black-haired, with a serious, calculating expression. He was said to be highly intelligent, and looking at him, she believed it.

She turned her attention to Empress Vitala, who had always fascinated her, not because of her looks—she was beautiful, as Nalica expected any empress would be—but because of her history. While she looked as southern Kjallan as her husband with her black hair and fine features, she'd been born and raised in Riorca, an impoverished province in the north that had spent decades rebelling against the empire. As a girl in Riorca, Vitala had been trained as an assassin for their resistance movement. Now, after a palace coup and a bloody civil war, she was empress. She'd proven to be an outspoken advocate both for Riorca and against slavery everywhere in the empire. Last year, she and her husband freed all the slaves in the Kjallan palace.

Nalica knew Vitala didn't care two tomtits about her, yet on some level she perceived the empress as her ally. Vitala, too, was a fighting woman.

The imperials were in position. A bugle sounded to begin the third and final round of the tournament. The crowd fell silent as an official explained the rules, for anyone who hadn't heard that speech the first two times. Nalica tuned him out. She ran through some exercises to limber up her muscles, and counted butts from the end of the row to locate her target. They were shooting at two hundred and fifty yards today, a ridiculous distance for accuracy, but with her war magic she could handle it.

Today the tournament directors had stationed a signaler near the targets, behind a protective wall. He was to send up flares when the archers hit their targets, for the benefit of those audience members who couldn't see at that distance.

She pulled an arrow from the stand and nocked it, trying not to look at Justien. He stood on her left in the lineup, and since she was left-eye dominant and he was right-eye dominant, it was unavoidable that they should face each other while shooting. Justien caught her gaze and gave her a curt nod. She nodded back and tried to put him out of her mind.

"Archers ready," called the official.

She stared at her distant target until her eyes watered. Raising her arm a little over her head to engage the powerful muscles of her back and shoulders, she drew her bow. War mages had a tendency to get lazy about form, because they got results even when they used their bodies inefficiently, but she was careful not to let that happen to her. One could not shoot one's best without good form.

"Loose."

Her arrow flew in what looked like a perfect arc. She lost sight of it during its flight and turned her attention toward the target. The arrow reappeared and slammed into the butt, landing quite close to the wand. A signal flare went up behind her target, and the audience cheered. She pumped her fist in triumph, and saw Justien do the same. He'd landed a hit too, but her arrow had landed closer to the wand. She had a good feeling about tonight. She was shooting well.

More flares went up. Three other archers had hit their butts. The rest, including Caellus, all had sins.

"Loose."

She sent her second arrow in another perfect arc toward the target and waited, dry-mouthed, to see if it would land. It did! Another flare. Her two arrows formed a neat horizontal row on the target. She glanced at Justien's target and saw two arrows there as well. She frowned. They were tied for the lead position.

She glanced up at the judges' stand and saw the emperor and empress leaning toward one another and talking. The empress was gesturing animatedly. Then the empress turned to the field of competition and looked straight at Nalica.

Their eyes met, and a shiver of fear and excitement ran down Nalica's spine. Her whole body felt electrified. She'd drawn the attention of the empress.

She licked dry lips and reached for her next arrow.

"Loose."

She let it fly and watched eagerly. Against competition this strong—Justien in particular—every shot mattered. She squinted at her target, praying for the arrow to arrive, and then there was an explosion of wood. Shards flew everywhere. She'd split the wand at two hundred and fifty yards.

Behind her target, a dozen flares went up at once.

The crowd roared. Joyous, she leapt into the air. Glancing up at the judges' stand, she saw the judges marking their score sheets, and the emperor and empress politely applauding. She grinned at the empress. Maybe that was forbidden—she was eastern Kjallan; what did she know of imperial etiquette?—but in her happiness, she couldn't help herself. The empress gave her a nod of acknowledgement.

Only then did she think to check her opponents' targets. Caellus had a hit, as did several others. But Justien had a sin this round. His expression was dark and stormy, and as he reached into the stand for his next arrow, he didn't meet her eyes.

Oh well. She wasn't responsible for his performance, only her own. And his mistake was to her advantage. She was now clearly in the lead. If she could just land her three remaining arrows, she would win.

"Archers ready."

She raised her bow. She didn't mind the stress of competition; she always performed well under pressure. The excitement of shooting in front of the emperor and empress was lifting her to her highest level of performance. Despite the adrenaline coursing through her, or perhaps because of it, her arms were rock steady, her bow absolutely still as she aimed and loosed her fourth arrow.

Another hit—she smiled in satisfaction. Two more and she would have that city guard job. Justien had scored a hit, but he was scowling. She understood why. It wouldn't be enough now for him to just hit the targets. Unless she missed one of her shots, he had to split the wand multiple times to beat her. And that wasn't likely at two hundred and fifty yards. She took another arrow and raised her bow.

"Loose."

She let her fifth arrow fly. Another hit, another flare. Nobody could beat her now, nobody! She was not going to miss with her final arrow. And even if Justien—who had another hit in this round—managed to split the wand with his final arrow, he still wouldn't beat her. Not unless she missed entirely.

"Loose."

She aimed carefully and sent her sixth and final arrow toward its target.

A hit! It was on the edge of the butt, but at this distance, that didn't matter. Any hit counted. She glanced at Justien's target. He had a hit too, but it wasn't enough. She had six, including a wand split, compared to his five. She had won the tournament.

She had thought she'd feel exuberant when this moment came, so full of energy and excitement that she could barely contain herself. Instead she was just relieved. It was said that the Vagabond smiled on those who risked everything they had in pursuit of a goal. Nalica had spent her last tetrals traveling to Riat, renting an overpriced room, and paying the entry fee for this tournament. She'd known she would have few options available to her if she lost. And the Vagabond had smiled: she'd won the city guard job, and her struggles were over.

Her whole body buzzed with nervous energy. Slinging her bow onto her shoulder, she paced, walking it off. She caught Justien eyeing her, looking none too pleased at having been beaten. She felt a little bad for him, but not much. He'd performed well, but she had outshot him fairly, and in this tournament there could be only one winner.

She only wished they could be together somehow, that she didn't have to say goodbye to him tonight.

He slung his bow over his shoulder and came to her, extending his arm. "Congratulations." His tone was a little grudging, but when she took his wrist, he clasped it warmly. "You'll make a wonderful addition to the guard."

"I'm sorry it cannot be both of us," she said.

He was the only competitor to acknowledge her victory. Caellus stared daggers in her direction, while the others simply averted their eyes.

The crowd was roaring. She'd apparently managed to tune that out until now. She turned and grinned at their obvious appreciation.

Captain Felix rose from his chair in the judges' stand and walked to the edge of the rail. He held out his arms, asking for silence, and the crowd quieted. "Citizens of Kjall, we have seen a fine exhibition over these three days of the Triferian. The Soldier himself should be pleased." He paused for a smattering of applause. "As you know, we have a special prize for the winner of this year's tournament: he— or she—will become a prefect in the Riat City Guard." More applause. "And now, citizens, the moment has come. I announce this year's winner, and the newest member of the guard. Please express your fondest appreciation for Justien Polini!"

Nalica blinked. Had she heard wrong? The crowd did not applaud, but lapsed into confused muttering.

Justien glanced at her, his eyebrows raised in bewilderment.

"Justien, if you'll come up to the judges' platform..." prompted Captain Felix.

As she began to comprehend what was happening, shock and horror stole over her. This wasn't a mistake. She'd been deliberately passed over. She'd won the tournament, but Captain Felix and the others didn't want her in the city guard. They wanted a man.

Justien glanced at her again as if desperate for help. Nalica just looked at him blankly. She had no idea what he should do.

In a halting voice, Justien spoke from the field, loud enough for the crowd to hear. "Sir, I think you may have made a mistake. Nalica Kelden outshot me."

Captain Felix's smile faded around the edges. "The winner is chosen at the judges' discretion."

Justien glanced back at her one more time, looking lost. She could see it in his eyes: he understood now. He knew that the judges had cheated her out of this win, and he was the lucky beneficiary of that cheating. He hadn't asked for this to happen, but now he would get the job and she wouldn't. She glared at him, hating him for that, even as she knew it wasn't his fault.

Behind her, the crowd began to boo. They didn't like this turn of events, either. She felt hot all over, knowing that her humiliation was being witnessed by so many people. She'd entered the tournament in good faith, believing she had as good a chance as anyone to win the prize. But she'd never had a chance at all.

She glanced up at the emperor and empress. Even they were witnessing this.

The empress was half out of her seat, with outrage written all over her face. A wild hope rose in Nalica as she watched. Might the empress overrule the judges' decision? Then the emperor rose and took his wife's arm. He spoke to her soothingly. The empress answered him—it looked like they were arguing—but in the end she took her seat. She looked displeased, but it was clear she wasn't going to interfere.

Nalica felt as if every eye in the crowd mocked her.

Justien turned to her and hissed, "I don't know what to do."

"Claim your prize," she said dully. "It's what you came for."

"I didn't want it to be like this."

"It's the judges' discretion. They don't want me." He might as well go up there and claim the job. Nothing would induce Captain Felix to hire her. She could have split the wand with every arrow, and it would have made no difference.

Oh gods, she'd agreed to congratulate him if he won. She held out her arm. "Congratulations."

He eyed her wrist without taking it. "I didn't win."

"Captain Felix says you did."

Captain Felix called out, "Justien Polini, come up and claim your prize."

After a last, frantic look in her direction, Justien walked to the judges' platform and ascended the stairs.

Nalica couldn't stand to watch any more of this farce. She unstrung her bow, leaned it on her shoulder, and walked away.

Justien's mind whirled. He had no idea what to do. His feelings were a nauseating mishmash of excitement, confusion, and horror at this unexpected turn of events. Nalica had beaten him. Every competitor on the field knew it, as did every member of the audience. Gods above, even the emperor and the empress knew! He'd fully expected

Nalica's name to be called, but when Captain Felix had called his instead, his mind had been upended, and now his thoughts and feelings were a shambles.

Everyone's eyes were on him, and the crowd was booing—which stung, frankly—and Captain Felix was calling him up onto the judges' platform to accept a prize that everybody knew he hadn't won. Could it be that he was wrong and the judges were right? In this tournament they weren't scoring in the standard way; instead, they'd left the determination of the winner to "judges' discretion." Maybe the judges had seen something in him that they hadn't seen in Nalica. They were choosing somebody to be a member of the city guard. Maybe they weren't interested just in accuracy, but in other factors.

Gods above, who was he kidding? The judges might have picked him because of "other factors," but he knew as well as anyone that the "other factors" were that Nalica was a woman and he was a man.

It shamed him to climb the steps, since it made him complicit in their crime. But what else was he to do? The audience's reaction, as he ascended, was a mixture of scattered applause and boos. His back stiffened. He wasn't a terrible shooter; not by any means. He'd shot second-best in the tournament, and his score had not been much lower than Nalica's.

Still, they knew. He had not won.

He glanced shame-facedly at the emperor and empress less than ten feet away. Their faces were bland and unreadable. He supposed they didn't think much of his "win" either. But they didn't seem inclined to interfere.

If he could muster the courage to walk all the way to Captain Felix, the job would be his.

He swallowed and forced himself to make those final steps. Captain Felix offered his wrist, and Justien clasped it. There were a few cheers from the audience. Also more boos. He looked down at the field of his competitors, searching for Nalica, but he couldn't find her. His heart ached. It was an awful thing Captain Felix had done to her, denying her the prize she had won fairly and with panache. He couldn't blame her if she couldn't stand to see it awarded to someone else.

Captain Felix spoke. "Welcome to the Riat City Guard, Justien Polini."

It ought to have been his moment of triumph, but he felt only the sting of shame. Amidst the confusion and the noises and the tumult of his emotions, he understood that he could not do this.

"Thank you, Captain," he said. The crowd quieted, and Justien's stomach roiled as he saw that every eye was on him. "Much as I would love to join the city guard, I cannot accept." There was a murmur from the crowd in response. In a shaking voice, he continued. "Nalica Kelden outshot me tonight. I didn't earn this win, and as an honest competitor, I must decline." He turned to the imperial couple to acknowledge them. "Your Imperial Majesties, thank you for this opportunity to compete."

Captain Felix looked stunned.

Justien glanced at the restless crowd. He couldn't stay here under all this scrutiny. He'd said his piece. If the judges were decent men, they would now reconsider their choice and give the prize to Nalica. He extricated his wrist from Captain Felix's grasp and descended from the platform back to the archery field.

Captain Felix addressed the crowd. "Since our winner declines the prize, the judges will confer and select a new winner."

The other archers brightened at this news, especially Caellus, since he'd shot better than most. The crowd continued to murmur as the three judges moved back from the stage and into a huddle. Justien remained on the field, shifting nervously from foot to foot. Where had Nalica gone? He hoped that if the judges did the right thing and gave her the prize, she could be found quickly.

The judges then separated, having finished their conference.

Captain Felix approached the railing to address the crowd once again. "Citizens, I would like to announce this year's winner of the archery competition and the newest member of the Riat City Guard: Caellus Atilian. Caellus, please ascend the stage to accept your prize."

Caellus yelped with joy and ran up the stairs. Justien watched with a sinking heart as Caellus and Felix clasped wrists. There was nothing more he could do. He'd given the judges a second opportunity to do the right thing, and they would not do it. They would never do it. Feeling as wrung-out as an old towel, he walked away.

Justien usually didn't worry about walking around the city of Riat at night. The imperial city was well policed and well lit. It didn't have a serious crime problem, and anyway he was a war mage. A common thug who tried to make a target of him would regret his foolishness. And yet Justien could not shake the feeling that he was being followed.

Footsteps echoed his own. He knew better than to stop short and make it obvious that he heard the other man, but when he slowed down, he could tell that the person following him took a moment to catch on before matching his speed. He sped up a little, and after a brief delay, the footsteps matched his speed once more.

Why would someone follow him? When Nalica had spotted that man in the brown syrtos who'd appeared to be following them at the festival, he hadn't taken the situation seriously. He was a war mage; it was impossible for an enemy to take him by surprise. But now he worried. Whoever was following him probably knew what he was. After all, he'd just come from the archery tournament. If this person knew what he was and was tracking him anyway, he might have the resources, or the numbers, to deal with Justien's abilities.

Justien kept to the main streets, avoiding alleyways. Even at night, it should be hard for someone to attack him in a public space. None of the moons were up yet, but light glows mounted on posts kept the streets reasonably bright. He moved from one circle of light to another, listening. Up ahead, patrons from a crowded all-night tavern spilled out into the street, singing and talking. He couldn't let his tail follow him all the way to Nalica's inn; that would put her in danger. He had to put an end to this, the sooner the better.

He stopped and turned on his heel. "Who's there?" he called. "I hear you following me." He scanned the streets, each darkened storefront, each alleyway. He could see no one.

A breeze from the harbor tickled his arms. He heard nothing. No footsteps, no anything. "What do you want?" he called again.

Several of the tavern-goers stopped to watch.

He turned and continued walking. This time he heard no footsteps at all.

By the time he'd reached the Crooked Billet, he felt certain he'd lost his tail. He wasn't sure that was the outcome he'd wanted, exactly. He'd have preferred a confrontation—preferably a nonviolent one—so that he knew who his follower was and what he wanted. The mystery remained unsolved.

He walked inside. His first thought was that the Crooked Billet wasn't good enough for Nalica. It was a dump. A few low tables housed some old men who nursed their ales without enthusiasm. The place looked clean enough, but it was dark and smelled of old, rotting wood.

The innkeeper approached him. "We're full tonight."

"I'm looking for a woman named Nalica," said Justien.

"Unless she's here in the common room, I can't help you."

Justien took a handful of quintetrals from his pocket and pressed them into the man's hand. "Perhaps this will change your mind."

The innkeeper slid the coins into his pocket. "Second floor, third door on the right."

Justien thanked him and ascended the stairs.

When the knock came at Nalica's door, she was annoyed. Her room at the Crooked Billet had offered her the first bit of privacy she'd had all day, and a safe place to let the tears flow after that disaster of an archery tournament. Now she was done with her foolish weeping, but the last thing she wanted was to talk with somebody. She was sick of the world and everyone in it.

She dragged herself off the straw tick, crossed the tiny room in a couple of steps, and opened the door.

Justien stood before her.

She blinked. What was *he* doing here? Maybe he'd come to gloat about his "victory," or else to renew his offer of supporting her on his city guard's salary. Either way, she wasn't interested. She started to close the door in his face.

He stuck his foot into the gap and stepped forward, pushing his way into the room. "Just give me a moment. I want to talk."

"What can you have to say? I know what happened. You won the 'tournament,'" she said, making no attempt to soften the contempt in her voice. "Go to your new friends, those crooked jack-scalders in the city guard. You've no business here."

He flinched as if she'd hurled arrows at him instead of words, and she noticed for the first time that he wasn't smiling and his eyes were dull and joyless. It appeared his "win" had not made him happy. Well, it shouldn't. He hadn't earned it.

"I'm sorry about what happened," he said.

Did she still have tear tracks on her face? She hoped not. "Sorry doesn't help. You've said your piece; now go. Big day tomorrow, starting the new job." She walked away from the door, hoping that would encourage him to leave.

"I didn't take the job," said Justien.

She turned, raising her eyes to his face. "Why not?"

"I hadn't earned it," he said. "I won't take what I haven't earned."

Fresh tears pricked the sides of her eyes. He hadn't taken the job? Her anger fled; that changed everything. But somebody had to take the job, and if it wasn't Justien...well, it clearly wasn't going to be her either. Unless the judges had changed their minds, and Justien had been sent to fetch her back? Could that be possible? "What happened when you turned it down?"

"They gave it to Caellus."

Her hope snuffed out like a candle flame. She sighed. "If they were looking for mediocrity, they got it."

"Mediocrity is what they deserve. You're too good for that job. So am I, frankly."

"I'm not too good for their tetrals."

"I know." Justien looked around her tiny room. "May I sit?"

She shrugged her shoulders. "Do as you please, but there are no chairs."

"How about on the bed?"

"All right. If you call that a bed." It was only a straw-stuffed tick laid on a wooden frame, but she at least knew after sleeping in it for three nights that it was free of lice.

He sat on the tick.

She paced about the small room, wishing she hadn't snapped at him earlier. She should not have doubted him. Deep down, she knew Justien was a good man. But she hadn't expected even a man as good as Justien to make such a sacrifice on her account. "Tell me everything. What happened after I left?"

"I wish I hadn't even gone up on the platform," he said. "I'd expected Felix to announce your name. I was preparing myself to applaud for you, even though I was jealous and angry with myself for missing the butt with that third arrow. And when he said my name instead, I was confused. I wondered if maybe I could have misunderstood the scoring. In the end, I went up there because he told me to and everyone was watching."

"I wasn't confused when it happened," she said, lowering her gaze. "Just humiliated."

"You've perhaps more experience with this sort of thing than I have," said Justien. "I know there's a certain antipathy toward women warriors, but I didn't think the judges would dare to be so blatant. Hundreds of people saw you outshoot me. Gods above, the emperor and empress saw it! And then I was called up on the platform to be supposedly honored—the crowd was booing, by the way."

"I heard them," said Nalica. "Much good it did."

"I felt trapped up there," said Justien. "But after I thought it over, I realized I couldn't accept the award. I told them you'd outshot me and I couldn't accept the prize. So I went back down to the field, and they conferred to pick a new winner. I was hoping they'd do the right thing this time and name you."

Her eyes swam, and her heart swelled with warmth. She wanted to hug Justien for standing up for her when no one else would.

"They didn't, though," he said. "Instead they named Caellus."

Now she hurt for Justien as well as herself. "I hate to say it, but in a way I wish you'd taken the job. Better you than Caellus, and they would never have given it to me."

Justien shook his head. "After what happened, I couldn't take it. And when I turned the job down, I felt *relieved*. Can you believe that? After wanting that job so badly, I was glad I wouldn't be stuck with it. Because I'd have known every single day that I didn't deserve it."

"Caellus deserves it even less."

"I know," said Justien. "I can't help that."

She went to the bed and sat beside him. "I wish I hadn't wasted my money on the entry fee. Maybe I should go back and demand that they return it. Obviously I wouldn't have entered if I'd known they wouldn't let me win."

"They won't give it back. If they did, they'd be admitting their deceit."

She sighed. "Captain Felix—that jack-scalder! I hope the authorities hauled him in and questioned him about the horse race, at least." She blinked. Was it possible she'd been passed over because of reporting his presence at the stable? No, probably not, otherwise Felix would have passed over Justien as well.

"He wasn't the only judge."

"They're all jack-scalders," she grumbled.

Justien raised a finger to her cheek and traced one of the old tear tracks. "I'm sorry it happened. I really am."

She turned away, flushing, and rubbed her face. But it wasn't his touch she objected to, and to make that clear, she scooted closer to him.

After a moment, he slipped an arm around her waist. "I almost forgot. I brought you a present." Metal clinked gently as he fished something from his pocket. "Here."

She opened her hand, and he poured a necklace into it. Sparkling yellow citrine winked up from her palm. She smiled. "From the jewelry tent."

"I figured if I was going to come here after what happened this evening, I'd better bring an offering. Let me put it on you."

She handed him the necklace and turned so he could fasten it around her neck. His hand on her tender skin sent a tingle all the way down to her toes.

"Thank you." She'd almost forgotten about the jewelry tent and this necklace. It was touching that Justien had thought to go back there and buy it for her.

Justien wrapped an arm around her. "Why don't we discuss what comes next."

She wriggled closer, leaning against his shoulder. "Nothing comes next. I'm paid at the inn through tonight. Tomorrow I'll leave town and look for work somewhere else. Riat is too gods-cursed expensive when you don't have a job."

"But you've no money to travel with."

She shrugged. "I'll get by. It's not the first time I've been broke."

"I'll be leaving town, too," said Justien. "There are no other jobs for war mages here; I've looked. I was thinking we could leave together."

She looked up at him. "Leave together and do what?"

"Look for work," he said. "As a team."

The idea had merit. Jobs for war mages were scarce, but most people hiring one at all needed several. Why not throw in her lot with Justien? They might struggle, but at least they would be struggling together. And there was no one else she'd rather be with.

"And maybe get married," he added softly. "If that appeals to you at all."

That was sudden. And yet the proposal was not unwelcome. Justien was the first man she'd met since leaving Vereth who felt right for her. She wished their financial future were not so uncertain, but this was the man she belonged with. Of that, at least, she was certain.

"There's no hurry as far as marriage is concerned," he said. "I just want you to know where I stand. I want you, but if you're not ready, I'll wait. You said you were out of money, but I've got some from my last job. I can keep us going long enough to find some kind of work, whether it's guarding a caravan or chopping wood. It'll be cheaper to buy one room on the road instead of two."

"I'm ready," she said. "Let's get married."

"Really?" he blurted. After a moment's stunned surprise, he hugged her so hard he stole her breath. "Until just now, this has been the worst evening of my life. And now it's the best."

She hugged him back. She might have lost the city guard job, but she didn't care so much anymore. Let Caellus have it.

"How do you want to do it?" asked Justien. "Big ceremony?"

She thought of her family at home and how horrified they would be that she was marrying a Polini. She tried to imagine a wedding in which both Keldens and Polinis were in attendance. That was not going to work. "No ceremony. Let's just find a clerk and sign the papers."

"Think we could find one right now?"

"I'm sure they're all in bed." Her eyes met his. She'd like to be in bed too. Not just sitting on it the way she was now. She licked her lips. "We can do the paperwork tomorrow."

"All right." His breath quickened, and after a moment of silence, he said, "Your hair's still braided for competition. Shall I take it down?"

She swallowed and nodded. She was going to sleep with him, and it was going to be tonight. Why wait? Until a little while ago, the evening had been a disappointment, but the rest of it didn't have to be.

"Turn this way." He positioned her so he had access to her hair and picked up her braid. "You don't use a tie?"

"I just knot it at the bottom for competition. The goal isn't to be fashionable; it's to keep the hair out of my face."

"It looks nice," said Justien. "Still, I like it better down."

She felt him untie the knot at the bottom and separate the strands. He was gentle and meticulous with his unbraiding, far more so than she'd been herself when putting it up in the first place. She'd tossed the braid together carelessly, leaving a smattering of stray hairs that poked out. He sorted through them, returning the strays to their fellows.

She sighed with pleasure. It felt good, his hands on her hair. As he worked his way up, his hands brushed her neck and scalp. Finally he completed the task of unbraiding and lowered her long, unfettered hair onto her shoulders. "Do you have a comb?"

"I can fetch one." She hesitated, not wanting to get up and lose the feeling of his hands on her, but the thought of his combing out her hair was even more appealing. She rose and took a comb from her travel bag, then sat in the same position as before, edging close to his body.

He took the comb and worked carefully, lifting her tresses and combing them out from the bottom to work out the tangles, moving steadily upward. When he reached her scalp, he cradled her head with his other hand to steady it. The comb slid smoothly through her hair. She leaned in to Justien, suddenly aware of how tired she was and how stiff and achy, less from the exertion of the competition than from her tense unhappiness about it afterward. It felt good to be taken care of.

She was almost sorry when Justien finished. But then he turned her head, leaned in, and kissed her, and she wasn't sorry at all.

It occurred to her that Justien must be tense as well after the evening's activities. Perhaps she could do something about that. "Would you like a back rub?"

His brows rose. "Gods, yes."

"Let me get behind you."

They swapped positions on the straw tick, but physically it didn't work. He was too big for her to reach his shoulders with quite the angle she wanted. He needed to either sit on the floor, which looked uncomfortable, or lie flat on the bed. She decided on the latter.

She patted the tick. "Lie here. Face down."

He gave her a devilish smile. "As you command."

Despite his great size, he was agile. He maneuvered his bulk onto the tick with more grace that she thought possible. He dwarfed the tick, not to mention the bed, but that couldn't be helped; these rooms were meant for southerners.

Since there was no room for her to sit beside him, she climbed atop him, settling herself gently onto his bottom. "I hope you don't mind if I sit here."

"Nalica, you can ride me any time."

Her cheeks heated, but she dismissed the images those words summoned. There would be time for that later. She laid her hands on his shoulders. This was not going to be easy; his muscles were like iron. She made a few exploratory touches, and found that his tunic got in the way of her hands. She lifted the fabric. "Can we take this off?"

"Absolutely." He raised himself just enough for her to free the fabric and pull it off over his head.

His half-naked body was as beautiful as she'd imagined. War magic generally kept a man, or a woman, well-muscled and in good condition even if they did nothing more strenuous than stand guard or sit a horse all day. But if the war mage engaged in activities that built muscle—combat training, manual labor, that sort of thing—the effects of the magic were stronger still. Justien's broad back was the most perfect expanse of human flesh she'd ever seen. He was sleek and muscular. She ran her hands down his back for sheer appreciation. Then she leaned forward, placed her hands on his shoulders, and began to knead out the tension.

"Oh gods," he moaned. "I think you're the first person who's been able to do that properly."

"Is this common for you—a woman offering you a back rub?"

"No," he said. "But I can tell you there aren't many people, male or female, who could do what you're doing."

She believed it. His shoulder muscles, especially those in his drawing arm, were round and solid. It took all of her magically enhanced strength to work the knots out of them. Though it was not easy work, she enjoyed it. Engaging her magic was pleasant; it made her feel powerful. And she loved touching him and feeling him melt beneath her hands. When she'd softened up his shoulders, she worked her way down his back, loosening the tight muscles on either side of his spine.

He groaned as she released each muscle in turn. Then he said, "I heard you were once engaged to marry. Back east."

"You've a good memory." She found a particularly troublesome knot and worked it with her thumbs, feeling him grunt and shift beneath her.

"It must not have led to anything. What happened?"

"Nothing exciting," she said. "It was an arranged marriage between clans, but there was a quarrel between clan members. The quarrel had nothing to do with me or him, but the marriage was called off."

"Do you ever regret it?"

"Not in the least." She worked her way down to his hips. These weren't so heavily muscled. She massaged them gently, and his flesh jumped beneath her fingers. Apparently he was ticklish.

"Gods, woman, you'll drive me crazy." Justien lifted his great body, forcing her to slide off him. "It's your turn. Let's swap positions."

She took his place on the straw tick, lying face down. He climbed atop her and rested gently on her backside, taking some of the weight on his knees so he didn't crush her. He tugged at her leather vest. "May I take this off?"

"Go ahead." She lifted her chest just enough to undo the ties in front, and let him slip it off her. Then he tugged the undershirt over her head. She sighed with relief as her breasts fell free from the confining material. She always wore tight shirts when shooting to keep her bosom from interfering with the action of the bow.

Justien's big hands went to work on her neck and shoulders. She groaned, first with pain as he dug deep, and then with an almost orgasmic relief as he loosened up muscles that had been tight since—well, for as long as she could remember. She sank boneless into the tick, ceding all control to Justien, trusting him fully.

"No one ever goes deep enough," he said. "You know what I mean?"

"I know exactly what you mean." He found a particularly good spot, and she added, "Oh, gods. Do that some more."

He complied.

"Did you have a woman back east, before you left?" she asked.

"Nothing serious," he rumbled.

He would have been an adolescent at that time. She wondered about the years following his departure from the east. He was strong, charming, and handsome; he would not have had trouble finding partners if he wanted them.

As if anticipating her next question, he continued. "I'll tell you the truth, Nalica. There haven't been many women. Those years in the battalion—I don't like to talk about this, but there were, uh, ladies of the night who followed the battalion from place to place. That sort of arrangement has never interested me. I am...how do I say this? I don't like to share."

"I understand that." She didn't like to share either.

He'd softened up the muscles along her back. Now he stroked her gently, as if in apology for the trauma he'd inflicted. The pain of the deep massage was fading, to be replaced by a feeling of blissful relaxation. He moved his hands lower, stroking her sides. His fingers brushed the sides of her breasts, and she felt herself twitch. That was an entirely different kind of sensation. She'd been halfway to falling asleep, he'd relaxed her so much, but now her body rekindled. Once again she wanted his touch, but in a different way.

"Later, when I was doing odd jobs," he said, still lightly stroking her and occasionally teasing the curve of her breast, "I didn't spend much time with women either. Sleeping with a stranger has never been something that interested me. And I moved around so much there was hardly an opportunity to get to know someone." He lifted his body, giving her room to maneuver. His voice had turned husky. "Turn over."

"Yes, sir." She twisted over onto her back.

His hungry gaze took in her half-naked body and lingered on her breasts. "I want you, Nalica. If you don't want this, you'd better say something right now. In a little while I won't be able to stop myself."

"I don't want you to stop."

"Are you warded?" he asked.

She nodded. "I had my wards done in Riat."

"Mine aren't so recent, but they're still good." He reached for her pants and undid the ties. She helped him draw them off her legs and drop them on the floor. His eyes followed her, reverent, and he made a small noise of appreciation. "You're the most beautiful woman I've ever seen."

"According to you, you haven't seen many," she teased.

"I don't need to, when I know exactly what I want." He touched the ties on his own pants. "Get these."

She unknotted his belt and pulled down his pants. As he kicked them down to the floor and settled himself atop her, she looked on his fully naked body. He was ready for action, his cock thick and erect, cods drawn up tight. He was as big as his body size had suggested he would be.

"Like I said, it's been a while," said Justien. "This first time, I don't think I can be gentle, and I might not last long. I'll make it up to you, I promise, hopefully on a number of occasions—"

"That's all right. I don't think I'll last long either." She didn't care if he wasn't gentle. She liked it a little rough.

He moved atop her and slid himself in. He was a tight fit, but she was wet and ready. As he slid home, she groaned. He felt right for her, exactly right.

He thrust once, slowly. "Gods above," he moaned. "Not going to last long at all."

She didn't answer, couldn't answer. He felt so good inside her. He was big and powerful, and he was all around her, arms and legs framing her. Her own significant size did not diminish her desire to feel engulfed by a man, to feel protected and cherished, safe and loved. She closed her eyes, giving herself over to the sensations as his movement accelerated.

She could tell he was holding back, that he was trying to be gentle this first time. But his gentleness was a slow torture; her body demanded more. "Faster," she said. "Please."

He responded with a burst of pent-up energy that made her cry out, and she realized just how much he'd been holding back. Pleasure spiraled through her as he thrust more forcefully. His mouth covered hers, and his hand found her breast. Suffused in sensation, she lost awareness of everything, of the inn's walls around her, the straw tick beneath her. There was only Justien, inflicting the most delicious violence upon her body.

"Almost there," she gasped.

He grunted, incapable of speech.

A feeling unlike any other radiated from her core, and she groaned, lost to it. Her body shuddered from her toes to the tips of her fingers, and he moved with her, stiffening and crying out as he reached his own climax.

There was a moment of stillness as they panted together on the tick. Justien was still inside her, and she floated through a haze of pleasant nothingness, drunk on sex.

As their breathing returned to normal, Justien kissed her gently and shifted his bulk so he was lying beside her instead of atop her. The tick was hardly big enough for one of them, let alone for both, and yet they made it work, fitting their bodies together like cogs in clockwork, holding each other tight.

Nalica slept dreamlessly in Justien's arms all night and through part of the morning. Then she awoke, quite suddenly, to someone pounding on her door.

5 After

Nalica rolled out of bed and in an instant was yanking her clothes on. Justien was on his feet too, surprisingly silent for such a big man.

The pounding at the door, which had paused, now resumed. She had the impression there were several people in the hallway. Voices rose and fell behind the door as they talked amongst themselves. Justien glanced at the door and wrinkled his brow as if trying to make out the muffled words. Then he grabbed his pants and slinked in the opposite direction to the window. He cracked the shutters and peered out into the streets.

"I see six horses," he whispered. "And a man who stayed behind with them."

That left five at her door. She pulled her shirt on. "Who do you think it is?"

"I've no idea," said Justien. "The man outside isn't wearing a uniform."

Nalica grabbed her vest, threw it over her shoulders, and fastened the ties.

"Visitors from the Imperial Palace," called a deep-voiced man. "Open the door."

"Just a moment," Justien answered him. "We're getting dressed."

The voices behind the door fell silent. Nalica tucked in her shirt and smoothed her clothes, hoping she looked presentable despite the wrinkles. If she'd known she'd have company this morning other than Justien, especially someone from the palace, she'd have hung up her clothes last night instead of leaving them in a sad pile on the floor.

Justien finished putting on his shirt. "Stay behind me," he said as he went to the door.

Nalica smiled. She didn't need protection, but it was kind of him to offer it.

Justien opened the door, and a man almost as big as he was came inside, looking alertly about the room. A second man and a woman followed him. They wore the silk syrtoses of the very rich or powerful. The men were armed with swords and pistols, and she could tell by the way they carried themselves that they were confident and experienced warriors. She had the impression they were bodyguards. She expected two more people to come in, based on the number of horses outside, but these did not materialize. Perhaps they waited downstairs.

The woman, dressed in red and gold silk, came forward and offered her arm. "My name is Kolta. I bring news from the palace and a proposition for you."

Nalica clasped wrists with her, and Justien did the same.

"Take a seat, if you will," said Kolta. "We need to talk."

The woman spoke as if command came naturally to her, and while she hadn't stated her rank or said anything about who she was aside from her name, it was clear that she was a lady of some importance. Nalica glanced around the room. Kolta had asked her to take a seat, but there weren't any chairs. She sat on the bed, and Justien settled beside her, folding his hands on his lap.

"There aren't any chairs in here," remarked Kolta in a tone of mild vexation.

"I'll fetch one," said a bodyguard. He hurried out the door.

Kolta addressed Nalica and Justien. "I want you to know that the imperial guard took Captain Felix Hadrianus of the Riat City Guard into custody last night and interrogated him. Under the influence of a truth spell, he confessed to poisoning one of the horses slated to run in the Imperial Plate. Fortunately, the poison was not a fatal one, and the animal will recover."

Nalica blinked. She was glad to know the fates of Felix and the horse, but she couldn't imagine why an imperial representative would come all this way to tell her about it. "Will the race be run again?"

"In a month," said Kolta. "The affected horse needs time to recover his condition."

"I'm glad to hear that the horse will have a second chance," said Justien.

The bodyguard returned, carrying a simple wooden chair. He placed it on the floor next to Kolta, and she took a seat. "I thought you'd like to know about the arrest since you were the ones who reported Felix's presence in the racing stables," said Kolta. "Without that tip, we wouldn't have known to speak to him."

"What will happen to Felix?" Nalica asked.

"He'll face trial," said Kolta. "I expect he'll receive twenty lashes and be removed from his position. The emperor won't allow a criminal to lead the city guard."

"Who will replace him?" asked Justien.

"The mayor will choose somebody." Kolta waved a hand, dismissing the subject. "That was quite a spectacle last night. The archery tournament, I mean."

It had been a fiasco, but Nalica wasn't going to say that in front of an imperial representative.

"What did you think of the outcome?" Kolta's eyes traveled from Nalica to Justien and back again.

"Were you present?" asked Justien.

"I was," said Kolta. "I saw everything."

"Then I believe you have some idea how I felt about it." Justien swallowed. There was a quaver in his voice that wasn't typical of him. "The judges passed over Nalica, and I'm sure it was because she's a woman. I declined their prize because I didn't want what I hadn't earned."

"I'm glad you turned it down," said Kolta. "A job in the Riat City Guard wouldn't have suited you. Nor would it have suited Nalica. You're too good for it."

Nalica hoped her pique did not show. This pampered scion of the imperium clearly had no idea how hard it was for a war mage, *too good* or not, to find work. "Thank you. But I'd have been glad to have that job. I wish I had won it."

"Why do you want the job?" asked Kolta. "Are you out of work? Please tell me about your backgrounds, both of you. I'm most curious."

Nalica glanced at Justien, who gestured at her to go first.

She took a deep breath while she collected her thoughts. This was starting to sound like a job interview. Clearly Kolta had an interest in them, and it had to be a serious interest for her to have come all this way. Maybe she was looking for another bodyguard, although the two she already had seemed more than up to the task. "I'm from Clan Kelden in Vereth province. That's mountain country, in the east."

Kolta nodded. "I'm familiar with Vereth."

"My people were herders," she continued. "When meat and milk prices dropped too low, we sold off our stock and formed a mercenary troop. I became a war mage at the age of sixteen. When my father grew ill and infirm, I took over leadership of the troop and ran it for five years. But the demand for mercenaries has dried up, and last year the troop disbanded due to lack of sufficient contracts. I've been looking for work ever since."

Kolta turned to Justien. "And you?"

"I'm Polini clan, also from Vereth province," said Justien. "When my family sold off their stock, I joined Red Eagle battalion as a prefect."

"Oh, I'm sorry. The emperor disbanded that one," said Kolta. "I take it you lost your position."

"Yes," said Justien. "Since then, I've been looking for steady work, but I've only been able to pick up short term assignments. Guarding dignitaries, escorting caravans, that sort of thing."

"The emperor had no choice about Red Eagle," said Kolta. "But believe me, he's aware of the difficulties that decision caused. Did either of you fight for or against the Usurper?"

Nalica shook her head. The woman was referring to the time several years before when a rival had temporarily seized Lucien's throne, leading to a civil war as Lucien and the Usurper raised armies and clashed. That had been a good time for her, in that there had been a lot of jobs available, but she had not been involved directly in the war.

Justien said, "I'm sure I would have fought on one side or the other if I'd still been in Red Eagle, but only the existing battalions were called up."

Kolta shifted on her chair, straightening the pleats of her syrtos. "Let me now get to my proposition. Allow me to introduce you to a couple of people." She gestured toward the hallway, and two more men entered the room. They folded their arms and stood in front of the open door.

One of them was a stranger, but Nalica recognized the other. "I know you!" she blurted. "You were following us at the Triferian." Though dressed in green today, he was the man she'd seen in the brown syrtos at the festival.

He smiled sheepishly. "Indeed, I was following you."

"Meet Lurio and Novius," said Kolta. "They are members of an organization called the Order of the Sage, which I am intimately involved with."

Nalica's brow furrowed. She'd never heard of it.

"This organization set them to following us?" asked Justien.

"I set them to following you," said Kolta. "I assigned a tail to every competitor in the archery tournament. The Triferian is a great opportunity for my agents to practice tailing people in large crowds without being noticed. Lurio is experienced. He was Nalica's tail, and I don't think either of you spotted him. Novius was recruited only a few months ago; he's still learning. I assigned him to Justien, and he told me you marked him twice."

"Once," said Nalica. "On Sage's Day."

"I marked him a second time last night," said Justien.

"He'll do better next time," said Kolta. "The other reason I had you followed is that I need more agents for the Order of the Sage. I particularly need war mages, and I particularly need women."

Nalica's stomach fluttered. She hoped this was going to be a job offer, but she didn't want to exclude Justien. "What exactly is the Order of the Sage?"

"You won't have heard of it," said Kolta. "It's new, established only a couple of years ago. And it's a secret organization, at least for the time being. The Order's mission is to promote peace throughout the empire, which is why it's named for the Sage.

"I had you tailed because I wanted to learn more about you. Obviously, I could evaluate some aspects of your battle prowess by watching the archery tournament, but combat skill isn't all I'm looking for in my Sage recruits. I need people who are versatile and intelligent, and above all, loyal to the imperial throne." She gave them each a penetrating look. "What can you tell me about your relationship to the imperium?"

Kolta's eyes came to rest on Nalica, and she took that to mean she was expected to speak first. What could she say? She was an easterner. Imperial politics were so distant from her life as to be an abstraction.

"My lady," she said, "I have spent most of my life in the east herding goats and leading a mercenary troop. From day to day, my concerns have been conflicts with rival clans and making sure my people had enough to eat. I know that for a person such as yourself, these concerns will seem trivial. I confess that in my humble life, I've had almost no awareness of the happenings at the imperium."

"An honest answer. Do you have any grievances with the empire?"

"No, ma'am."

Kolta turned to Justien. "How about you? I imagine you harbor some resentment over the disbanding of your battalion."

"Yes, ma'am," he said. "But I understand that it was disbanded for financial reasons. I was sorry to lose my job, but I know the empire cannot pay soldiers with money it does not have."

"At least you did not turn to banditry afterward. Some of your fellows did."

Justien nodded.

"Kjall is a far-flung empire," said Kolta. "I perfectly understand that most of its people are too busy living their lives to concern themselves with imperial politics, and when they do, they may have limited information, which may lead them to draw poor conclusions. I cannot evaluate your loyalty to a group of people you barely know, and it would be unfair of me to try. Therefore what I look for in my Sage candidates is honesty and general trustworthiness.

"I know that the two of you reported seeing Captain Felix in the stables when you knew that doing so could have unfortunate consequences for yourselves. I know that Justien declined the archery win he badly wanted because he knew he had not earned it. I am impressed with your character, both of you, and I would like to offer you positions as agents in the Order of the Sage."

Nalica exchanged a glance with Justien. This was it: the job offer. But she wasn't sure how excited she ought to be. She had no idea what it meant to be an agent in this organization. "You say your agents promote peace within the empire. What exactly do they do to accomplish that?"

"Gather intelligence," said Kolta. "If rebellion is brewing in a distant corner of the empire, the emperor needs to know about it before violence breaks out. If an official is corrupt and treating his people cruelly, the authorities must be informed so that they can remove him from power."

"We'd be spies?" asked Justien.

Kolta's brow furrowed. "That's not far off the mark, but my agents don't operate overseas. For the time being, it's a domestic organization."

"Can you give us some idea of what we'd be doing on a day-to-day basis?" asked Justien.

"First you'd have to spend some time in training," said Kolta. "Do either of you know any languages besides Kjallan?"

Nalica and Justien shook their heads.

"We'd remedy that at once," said Kolta. "My agents must be multilingual. If you join us, you'll spend the next year or two at the imperial palace, filling in the gaps in your education and learning the skills you'll need in order to operate successfully undercover. When you've completed your training, I'll assign you a post somewhere in the empire. Ostensibly you'll be serving as some sort of imperial representative, but that job will be a cover. Your primary task will be to gather information."

"You want war mages," said Justien. "Does that mean you anticipate fighting?"

"I don't anticipate any at all," said Kolta. "But it pays to be prepared. If my agents uncover trouble, I want them to be in a position to handle it."

"Will we have to assassinate people?" asked Nalica.

"No," said Kolta. "But I have the authority, which I grant to my agents, to make arrests and bring people to trial."

"How much would we be paid?" asked Nalica.

"While you're in training, two hundred tetrals per month. Once placed in the field as an agent, five hundred tetrals per month."

Nalica gasped, and Justien sat up straighter.

"I pay my agents generously for a reason," said Kolta. "I find it goes a long way toward ensuring their loyalty."

"Are there any downsides to this job?" asked Justien.

"Many," said Kolta. "My agents go where I want, when I want them to, without exception. You will live where I post you, and you could be moved at any time. You will swear an oath of fealty to me under truth spell, and you may be asked to renew that oath periodically. You may have to perform some duties you find unpleasant, like interrogating prisoners. And the minimum term of service is twenty years."

Nalica swallowed. Twenty years, and no freedom of movement. She and Justien had just agreed to marry—but if they joined the Order, they could be posted to different parts of the country. If she took this job, would she have to give up Justien?

Kolta's gaze pierced her. "What's on your mind? You look unhappy."

"Well..." She slipped her hand into Justien's. "Do you ever have agents who work as a team, such that wherever one is posted, the other is posted too?"

Kolta smiled and leaned back in her chair. "I had a feeling you two were a couple; your tails ran into each other last night. Have you been together long?"

"We're getting married," said Justien.

"Good," said Kolta. "Do it. Married couples are easy to place undercover and less likely than singles to arouse suspicion. Once you're married, I'll post you as a team."

Nalica hated to ask for more—the offer was so generous already, and she could hardly imagine turning it down. But she might not have the opportunity to speak to this spymistress again after this morning, and she figured it was best to lay all her cards on the table. "May I have children? Or is that forbidden to your agents?"

"You certainly may have children," said Kolta. "But I'll require you to hire a full-time nurse to look after them, in case you're needed in the field on short notice. Your salary should more than adequately cover that expense."

Justien slipped an arm around Nalica and squeezed.

"Any more questions?" asked Kolta.

"What happens if we say no?" asked Justien.

"In that case, I'll fetch a mind mage and she can use a quick forgetting spell on you," said Kolta. "You'll wake up here and have no idea this meeting took place."

A shiver ran down Nalica's spine. She supposed it had to be that way, to keep the organization secret.

"Think it over before you decide." Kolta rose from her seat. "Joining the Order of the Sage is no small commitment. You'd be in my service for the next twenty years. There is no changing your mind halfway. Do you understand?"

Nalica and Justien nodded.

"I'll wait outside the door." Kolta left the room, accompanied by Lurio and Novius and the two bodyguards.

The door closed behind her, and Nalica and Justien were left alone.

A shudder ran through Justien from head to toe. "Three gods. Did you recognize that woman?"

"No. Should I have?"

Justien lowered his voice. "That was the empress."

Nalica glanced at the closed door. The empress of Kjall? Surely not. Yes, there was a superficial resemblance. Kolta was black-haired like the empress, and of similar height and build, but lots of Kjallan women shared those traits. "I'm sure you're wrong."

"No, I'm right," said Justien. "You just talked to the empress of Kjall."

Nalica shook her head in wonder. Maybe he *was* right. Maybe the empress preferred to move about town undercover, without that horde of Legaciatti around her, attracting attention. It didn't matter. The job offer was the same.

Justien grinned. "Well, what do you think? Aren't you glad you didn't win the archery tournament?"

She laughed, but not purely for joy; her nerves were frayed, and she was giddy, a state of mind she didn't trust. In less than a day, she'd received both a marriage proposal and the most generous job offer of her life. She felt as if she were standing on a precipice, looking down at certain death while a voice whispered in her ear, *Jump! You'll fly.*

"Shall we accept?" asked Justien.

"I don't see how we could do anything else," said Nalica.

"That's how I feel about it. But don't you find it a little bit frightening?"

"I find it a lot frightening."

Back east, as the young daughter of the clan lord, Nalica had thought herself a person of importance, but as the years had passed, she'd come to understand the reality of her situation. She was important within the clan, but the clan was a tiny organization, of local importance only, unknown and ignored by the rest of the world. Later, the clan's dissolution had forced her to take a broader perspective. She'd learned how much bigger the rest of the world was, and she'd perceived, for the first time, her own insignificance. It frightened her, but it also exhilarated her. The world was enormous, full of infinite variety and infinite opportunities.

"You look thoughtful," said Justien.

She took his hand and squeezed it. "I was thinking we've come a long way."

"Are we taking the offer, then?"

"Yes."

Justien wrapped her in his arms and kissed her. "Let's go tell the empress the good news."

THE END

NOTE FROM THE AUTHOR

Thank you for reading "Archer's Sin!" I hope you enjoyed it. This novella is a companion to my Hearts and Thrones series, which begins with the novels <u>Assassin's Gambit</u>, <u>Spy's Honor</u>, and <u>Prince's Fire</u>. Chronologically, Nalica's and Justien's story takes place between the events of <u>Assassin's Gambit</u> and <u>Prince's Fire</u>. (<u>Spy's Honor</u> is a prequel.) Don't be surprised if these characters show up again in <u>Prince's Fire</u> and other books...

If you'd like to know when my next book is available, you can subscribe to my newsletter at http://www.amyraby.com, or follow me on Twitter at @amyraby, or like my Facebook page at https://www.facebook.com/Amy.Raby.Author.

I appreciate all reviews, whether positive or negative. Please consider leaving an honest review at Goodreads or your favorite retailer.